The Murderer's Tale

The Murderer's Tale

Margaret Frazer

ROBERT HALE · LONDON

© Gail Frazer, 1996
First published in Great Britain 2012

ISBN 978-0-7090-9596-5

Robert Hale Limited
Clerkenwell House
Clerkenwell Green
London EC1R 0HT

www.halebooks.com

2 4 6 8 10 9 7 5 3 1

Typeset in 11/15pt Classical Garamond
Printed in the UK by the MPG Books Group

For this was outrely his fulle entente,
To sleen hem bothe, and nevere to repente

The Pardoner's Tale
Geoffrey Chaucer

Chapter 1

BEYOND THE GREAT hall's high-set windows the night had begun to grey toward the coming dawn. Giles, seated at the far end of the dais steps and leaned back on his elbows with his legs stretched out at ease in front of him, watched the roof beams take black shape in the greying dark above him. He knew he would soon be visible to the servants at their shift and hurry along the hall's far side between the lamplit stairs and the porchward glow of the torches in the yard where the horses were being readied for the day's ride, but for this while more the darkness hid him and he could watch their come and go unseen himself.

The main baggage had been finished with yesterday and was probably long since roped onto the carts that would groan out of the yard as soon as it was light enough to see the road. In the normal way of things they and most of the servants would have been gone a full day ago, to have the Langling manor ready before the household arrived, but there was no need to be that forward this time. The household would be days behind them – damn Lionel and his pilgrimages. The yearly move from Knyvet where they had been since Martinmas, to Langling each spring – and then back to here to Knyvet come late autumn again – was trouble enough for just about everyone. But not for Lionel who had to waste his prayers and money and everyone's time going widdershins through half-a-dozen counties to shrines that almost no one else ever bothered to hear of.

At least at the great pilgrimage places there had been amusements to be had, but now that the Virgin Mary and St Thomas Becket and the holy blood of Hailes and their ilk had failed him, Lionel had turned to lesser places, to out-of-the-way shrines of out-of-the-way saints where there was nothing to be had but prayer and boredom. And all to no purpose.

But Lionel would not give up. Not him. He still clung to his idiot hope that he would be cured and could not see that if these saints he was bent on now were any good, they would have something more to show for it than crock-sized chapels on back roads.

Giles sat up and stretched his arms forward, easing his shoulders. At least along the way this year there would be a few days at Lord Lovell's. Belatedly, after a three-years lapse, Lionel's overlord wanted to see how well or – more to the point – how ill Lionel was doing, and Lord Lovell kept a goodly table and had been rebuilding Minster Lovell these past years so there should be good eating and some comforts at least.

Unfortunately the church at Minster Lovell was dedicated to St Kenelm, and that had given Lionel the notion to go on pilgrimage not only there but to St Kenelm's shrine and grave at Winchcombe Abbey and then, God help it, to the six other smaller churches dedicated to him which were scattered around this only corner of England that bothered with so nobody of a saint.

Leave it to Lionel, Giles thought, to go chasing down the relics of a boy-king murdered hundreds of years ago for no more holy purpose than that his sister was ambitious and her lover compliant. Kenelm was not even known for curing the falling sickness so far as Giles had ever heard, and wasn't that supposed to be the purpose of all this?

But Lionel was long past reason in the matter and, come what might, to all seven shrines, no matter how miserable they were, he meant them to go before he was finished.

A servant coming off the bottom step from the stairs stumbled, probably over his own clumsy feet, and lost his grip on one side of the chest he was carrying. One heavy end thudded to the floor. The man cursed, both at the chest and at the laughter of one of his fellows coming behind him with a cloth-wrapped roll. Together they bent to see if there was any damage, then he hauled it back into his arms and they went on, laughing together over something.

Giles nodded to himself. There had been light enough to recognize Dickon, and time would come when Giles would have his holly stick to hand and Dickon in reach, and then Dickon would pay, with interest, for his carelessness and his laughter at it. Better late than never, though Dickon probably would not think so, and that – along with Dickon's yelps – would be part of the amusement.

Giles stood up. The windows were lightening with the growing day and time was come to see how things went above stairs.

Much as he had expected, he found. They were almost done. Servants were carrying the last of the baggage out of the parlour, and Lionel and that damned Martyn were standing by the table near the shuttered windows where what there was for breakfast this morning was laid out. The hardening ends of yesterday's loaves and the unspiced middle of last night's meat and likely only lukewarm ale in the pitcher when it should have been hot, spiced wine. A chill April dawn with nothing better to look forward to than a day's long riding was not his most favourite time; spiced wine would have helped his ill humour at least a little and made the meal palatable if not pleasurable. When he was master here – and God help him make Lord Lovell see it should be soon – things would be better ordered by a long way.

But for now everything was Lionel's and none of it was Giles's except for what Lionel allowed him. Everything except for Edeyn. She was the one thing of dear cousin Lionel's that Giles had taken for himself. The thought made him smile as he joined Lionel and Martyn beside the table, loathing the both of them as he did so. His long-jawed cousin could never seem to keep it in his head that Martyn was servant here, not master. They kept company together thick as thieves, Martyn always somewhere close to hand and no room left for Giles to work things the way he wanted them to go.

It had been like that for fifteen years now, ever since the first fit had come on Lionel. He had been fourteen then and Giles eighteen and glad to show his little cousin the way things ought to be. They had been in the stable yard, talking to Martyn who was only twenty but already acting like he knew more than all of them together just because his father was Lionel's father's steward, and some stable hands, and there had been nothing different to warn what was going to happen. One moment Lionel had been standing there, talking, laughing. The next he had been on the ground, gone down and unconscious like a struck ox. They had all stared at him, too startled to move. And then before they had their wits about them, he had begun to jerk, in spasms at first and then a wild writhing, grunting and with a froth at his mouth.

They had pulled back from him, bumping into each other in their haste, understanding now, crossing themselves in desperate protection against whatever fiend, demon, or demons had entered him and was fighting for his body.

Except for Martyn. He had jumped back with the rest of them sharp enough when Lionel began to writhe and gibber, but he was a knave in the grain even then. Already marked to follow his father as the steward of the Knyvet lands, he knew how to keep his bread buttered side up. Against anything like common sense, he had caught himself and, as everyone drew further back, went forward and down on his knees beside Lionel, trying to hold him still, to keep his head from battering against the cobbles, while yelling for someone to bring the priest.

Someone had grabbed back wits enough to run then, but the rest of them had just stayed frozen with horror, Giles included, watching Martyn trying to hold Lionel, praying out loud over him until finally the fit ended and Lionel lay there unconscious, slack, his bloodied head lolling in Martyn's hands.

The priest had finally come and plenty of other folk too. There had been no question of keeping the matter quiet. The master's heir had been taken by a demon in front of half-a-dozen men and that was too many mouths to keep shut. As it was, of all those who were there and came, no one had wanted to touch Lionel even when the fit was past. Only Martyn's angry orders had forced some of them – not Giles – to lift him, carry him inside.

By then some of the horror had eased. Martyn had had help to wash him, treat his hurts, put him to bed. He had looked to be no more than asleep then, but a sleep so deep that nothing wakened him. The priest had gone on praying over him, and eventually Lionel came conscious, dazed, exhausted, with no memory of anything between standing in the stable yard and waking in his bed.

He never remembered, not that fit or the very many others there had been since then. Giles had seen more of them than he wanted to and avoided as many as he could. That at least had become easier since Lionel had come to know the signs that one was coming. He used them for warning to withdraw to some-where alone except for Martyn. The demon might leave him alone for months at a time, but when it came on him it was vicious, and Martyn was the only person Lionel would accept near him. Come to that, it was only Martyn who wanted to be near him. Everyone else was more than willing to keep far away, because a man with demons trying to wrench his soul and body apart was more than just an ugly sight. He was dangerous, because who could guess where a demon might decide to go when it let him loose? Anyone near might be fair game.

But nearly always good old Martyn was there, trying to save damned Lionel from injury as much as might be and tend to him afterwards when he was exhausted, dazed, and sometimes hurt. Good old Martyn, who had thereby become more master than servant here when instead it should all have come to Giles.

For a while it had seemed that Lionel would lose his right to inherit because of his fits, and Giles had had hopes. As Lionel's cousin by Master Knyvet's younger brother, he was the next male heir of the blood and everything would come to him if Lionel were ruled unfit to inherit. But his uncle had gone to great legal lengths and great expense to protect and insure that Lionel would follow him. The waste of money and favours had set Giles's teeth on edge and, worse, now that his uncle was dead, he had to watch Lionel enjoy everything that could so easily have been his by now. Oh, he would have it some day, since Lionel was unmarriageable – both of his own choice and because no woman would have him, not even Edeyn – and therefore, since there would be no heirs of Lionel's body to succeed him, everything would come to Giles eventually.

It was the 'eventually' that irked.

That and having nothing of his own except a single manor with a broken-down hall and paltry lands, so that it was far more comfortable and convenient to live on Lionel's bounty than his own, even if it did mean watching Lionel have and spend what should have been his by now and might not be his for a long while yet to come because the fits did not kill, only tormented, more was the pity.

To make matters worse, Martyn had followed his father as steward of the Knyvet lands after his father died a year after Master Knyvet. Giles had had some thought that with his uncle and his uncle's steward gone he would have more hand in things, more influence over Lionel, some benefit from Lionel's curse, but first, last, and always good old Martyn was there and in the way.

He and Lionel were laughing now over something Giles had not heard as he entered, even while they turned from the table, done with their breakfast, to greet him.

'Giles! No one could find you,' Lionel said. 'We thought you'd started off without us. Have you eaten?'

'Not yet. I was out and about to see if everything was going on as it should be.' He had not been but they would not bother to ask anyone. The point of it was his glance at Martyn to show he thought it should have been Martyn out there instead of him, but Lionel missed his look, the way Lionel missed most of what Giles wanted him to see. It was Martyn who caught it clear enough and quirked a corner of his mouth in amused acknowledgement mixed with refusal to be drawn.

He was sharp, was Martyn. As sharp as Lionel was dull. And insolent, knowing how strong his hold on Lionel was, with no fear it ever being broken. Giles meant to break that insolence some day. To – just once but for always, please God – wipe that satisfaction off Martyn's face.

But it would not be now, and he joined them at the table with a smile, chose among the loaf ends for one not gone too dry and found a piece of roast that suited him, savory with a crust of herbs. But as he had feared the pitcher only held plain ale.

To make some use of the time he said, 'Dickon dropped one of the chests at the foot of the stairs just now. You might want to see if aught was damaged.'

Idly spearing a bit of meat with his dagger, Lionel said, 'Everyone knows Dickon is a ham-fisted simpleton.'

'So we see to it he's only given things to carry he can't damage,' Martyn added.

Giles shifted ground. 'What was so funny when I came in?'

Lionel grinned. 'A riddle. Martyn has a new one.'

Giles's belly lumped cold around the meat he had just eaten. Martyn and Lionel and their damned riddles. God knew Lionel's long-jawed face with its scar across brow and bridge of nose from when he had fallen against a lighted lamp in a sudden fit four years ago looked the better for laughter but those damned riddles....

He looked at Martyn matching Lionel's grin and managed to say evenly, 'A new one? I should have thought there was not a riddle left the two of you had not tried out. What, pray, is it?'

Lionel and Martyn exchanged a glance of shared amusement. 'You ask it,' Lionel said. 'It's yours.'

Martyn composed his face with the insolent assurance he had when showing how clever he was and said, gravely as a bishop questioning the Pope, 'Can you tell me what animal has its tail between its eyes?'

Giles looked from Lionel's face to Martyn's and detested both of them for knowing the answer and being sure he would not have it. An animal with its tail between its eyes? Whatever the answer was, it was going to be undoubtedly too stupid to have wasted his time over. 'I can't conceive. What animal has its tail between its eyes?'

Martyn grinnned. 'A cat licking its rump.'

Giles managed a credible laugh and granted, 'A good one. I'd never have thought of it.' And would never have wanted to.

'Don't tell Edeyn,' Lionel said. 'I want to see her face when I ask her.'

'I won't,' Giles assured him. He set what was left of his breakfast on the table, took a quick drink of ale, gave a quick bow of his head to Lionel and said, 'Speaking of Edeyn, I'd best see how she does. Pray, excuse me.'

Lionel excused him with insulting readiness.

Giles's pair of rooms lay the other way than Lionel's off the parlour. The outer one of them was bare today, stripped of its tapestries and cushions, the shutters closed and barred over the lower half of the windows where the glass panes had been removed to be packed for going to Langling. Their unshuttered upper halves showed full grey dawnlight and the last of the stars gone. The carts would be on their way shortly and so should the rest of the household.

As Giles crossed the room toward his bedchamber, one of his men came from the further doorway and circled hurriedly aside to make ample room for him to pass, bowing low while he did despite the small leather-bound box he carried in both arms.

Giles nodded at the chest. 'Is that the last of it?'

'Except for what Mistress Knyvet's maids will carry, master.'

'Then hurry up with it. We're behindhand in our going as it is and Master Lionel is impatient to be off.'

The man bowed again, shifting further aside and more quickly on his way.

In the bedchamber, Giles found Edeyn standing beside the stripped, unmattressed bed, her cloak over her arm, watching her two maids folding a thick cloth around her jewel box that would go in a saddle-bag for especial safe keeping. The maids did not look up as he came; they had heard what he said outside the room and their movements were earnest with hurry. But Edeyn smiled at him as he crossed to her. He took hold of her chin, lifting her face to him for a kiss he lingered over. He preferred large-breasted, wide-hipped women; they offered more for him to grasp in bed. Edeyn, alas, was completely opposite, small-boned and slender and hardly as high as his shoulder, but he had taught her how to kiss and do other things that pleased him and all in all they managed well enough.

Well enough that she was four months along with what would be his heir if it were a boy. The heir she would have gladly borne Lionel if Lionel's marrying had not been impossible.

Giles sometimes wondered if she knew that he knew she had loved Lionel before she loved him. He did not mind she had, was in fact glad of it. It made having her more pleasurable. And because he suspected Lionel had loved her in return, maybe still did love her, come to that, he made a point sometimes of letting Lionel see how very much Edeyn was now his. A word, a gesture, a casual mention of a particularly good night's work between them. Never much. Just a little paying back for everything else that Lionel had that should have been his.

As he drew back from their kiss, Edeyn smiled up at him and said, 'We're ready.'

'Good then. Let's be off. Lionel is waiting.'

She nodded obediently, obligingly, and moved away as her maids caught up the last of their own things. Giles let her reach the door before he said, 'Edeyn. One other thing.'

She turned back toward him. 'Yes?'

'Lionel has a new riddle.' Edeyn was forever trying to be part of Lionel and Martyn's riddle games, but she had more will than wit for them and her guesses were usually so far awry they made more laughter than the right one would have. 'When he asks you it, say it's a cat licking its arse.'

One more small put-paid to Lionel.

Chapter 2

THE GARDEN WAS still sweet from the late afternoon rain. A band of saffron-coloured sunset showed below the westward clouds, and the light lay long and golden over the garden wall, gilding where it touched. Along the paths crystal droplets pattered from low leaves, swept clear by the nuns' long skirts as they walked past in their evening recreation, two of them pacing side by side, hands folded into their sleeves, the third alone, her rosary in her hands. Above them, silhouetted against the yellow sky on the high arch of the pear-tree's branch beyond the wall, a thrush sang to the world. The garden was hushed to the soft sound of their walking, the rain droplets patter, the thrush's evening singing.

Loud laughter jarred into the quiet from the cloister beyond the garden wall. Frevisse and Dame Claire paused in their walking, their heads turning toward the noise, as if the gathering of the priory's other nuns could be seen, there in the warming room where they had chosen to spend the recreation hour in talk over the spiced, warm wine the prioress had allowed them against the April day's damp and alleged chill. Under Prioress Domina Alys's disapproving eye but allowed it by the Rule, Frevisse, Dame Claire, and Sister Thomasine had chosen instead to go out into the garden, forgoing both the wine and crowded talking for the quiet of the rain-sweet April evening.

But there was no real escape. The other nuns' jollity pursued them at least by ear, and at the end of recreation they must needs rejoin them for evening prayers and then to bed in the long dormitory, where often and often anymore the rule of silence did not hold, as it should by St Benedict's Rule that ordered silence all through the day except at need and in the hour of recreation. Instead the talk went on with giggling and whispering through the walls of the sleeping cells, keeping everyone awake and making it hard for them to rouse for the midnight prayers of Matins and Lauds.

Frevisse, turning away from the laughter, momentarily envied Sister Thomasine's serene detachment from it all. Untouched by the laughter, St Frideswide's youngest nun stood below the garden's outer wall, gazing up rapt at the thrush still singing to the heavens. In this spring of God's grace 1437, Sister Thomasine had been in St Frideswide's Priory seven and a half years, a nun for over five of those, and with no desire in her heart except to go on as deeply into worship of her Lord as she could manage, with no apparent thought at all of the tensions growing daily greater under the priory's newly fissured peace.

Time was when Frevisse had found the child very tedious, but an unworldly maturity as well as womanhood had grown on Sister Thomasine through the years. Her mind always bound to God and her prayers, she nonetheless went about her duties through the nunnery with a quiet efficiency, made probably more quiet and efficient, Frevisse admitted, because she was so detached from them. Quite against her inclination Frevisse had come to – not affection; Sister Thomasine's earnestness still wore at her nerves too frequently – an acknowledgment of her deep though different worth and, lately, her envied ability to live untouched beyond the changes Domina Alys as prioress had wrought in St Frideswide's these past seven months.

Dame Claire sighed and walked on. Frevisse went with her,

shortening her stride to match Dame Claire's lesser with the ease of long familiarity.

'You know what she thinks of our being out here,' Dame Claire said.

There was no question of whom she meant. Domina Alys was too much in their minds just as she was too much in their lives. 'That we're talking of her,' Frevisse said. 'Which we are.'

'More than that. Worse than that. She thinks that we're plotting against her. Sister—' Dame Claire stopped, her hesitancy telling a great deal about the wariness now become part of the priory's life. 'That's what someone told me. That she thinks whenever we come out and the others stay in, we're plotting against her.'

'Plotting what? She's prioress, God help us all. What can we do?'

Frevisse did not try to conceal her irritability. Forbearance was not among the virtues she had sufficiently cultivated yet in her life, and Domina Alys's overbearing ways were an unceasing trial to her, most simply because under obedience to the vow she had taken almost twenty years ago when she became a nun, she was pledged to obey without hesitation or grudging those whom God put over her. Until last summer that vow had been no trouble to her because Domina Edith had been prioress when she made it. Domina Edith who had been kind and wise with years, with a knowing eye and a steadying discipline on the women given into her care – women as different from one another as any group of women anywhere despite their common bonds of avowed nunhood, their shared hours of prayer seven times a day, their enclosure within St Frideswide's walls, and their black Benedictine habits and veils, the white wimples encircling their faces, that gave them an outward sameness. While Domina Edith was their prioress, a balance had been kept, with no overt favourites, no choosing one nun over another for this duty or that privilege except as they had deserved or earned it, and a fair, strict keeping of St Benedict's holy Rule for everyone.

But Domina Edith had died quietly of old age and her body's weariness last summer, and matters were different now. Dame Alys – *Domina* Alys – had a very different way of governing. Frevisse readily admitted the title still stuck in her throat, even now, seven months after the election. An election whose outcome had been a mistake, Frevisse still felt. If God allowed mistakes in such matters, she conscientiously added, and she rather thought He did, human pride and certainty should learn the lesson of their own fallibility.

It had been understood among the nuns, when Domina Edith was dead and they were bound to elect her successor from among themselves, that then-Dame Alys dearly coveted the honour and the power that went with it. Domina Edith's own choice had been Dame Claire, known to be steady, fair-minded, given to deep concern for those in her care when she was the priory's infirmarian and later its cellarer. Frevisse thought that very likely Dame Claire would have had the election if matters had gone sensibly, but Dame Alys had a temper that boiled quickly and held onto wrongs long, and so near as Frevisse had been able to sort out, most of the nine nuns had been wary, if not plain afraid, of Dame Alys's temper and memory. None wanted her as prioress but some of them had been fearful of what would have to be endured if she received not even a single vote on the first ballot. Frevisse herself had not cared; she had cast her vote willingly for Dame Claire, and so had Sister Thomasine, she thought, because Sister Thomasine was unswayed by such worldly troubles as fear of Dame Alys's wrath. Frevisse herself had received one vote – from Dame Claire, she knew – and had been glad to have no more. But the other six votes had all gone to Dame Alys, because Dame Alys had, of course, voted for herself and each of the other five nuns had thought to give her just one vote on the first ballot to appease her after-wrath a little.

Instead, out of their cowardice, they had given her the election and now, for the length of her life, she was prioress of St Frideswide's.

More laughter broke across the evening's quiet. Most of the nuns had made a kind of peace with what had been wrought. Frevisse had to admit that. It was undeniable that so long as Domina Alys had her own way, she could be pleasant to those under her. But her own way often went astray from the Rule toward indulgence and slackness. A little sleeping late and prayers delayed on cold winter mornings, small, needless luxuries of food on non-feast days; warmed, expensively spiced wine for no good reason except she felt like it.

Little things. Always little things, but more and more of them and beginning to be bigger things. Today in the morning's chapter meeting, Sister Amicia had asked if they could not all be allowed to stroll abroad, outside the nunnery, that afternoon. 'Just a little way. It's spring,' she had said wistfully.

Sister Amicia was known for having more the worldly inclinations of a merchant's wife than the holy interests of a nun. A gentle but unrelenting hand needed to be kept on her, to keep her as she was supposed to be, and strolls abroad to see the world would, in the long run, do her more harm than good. Besides all that, her request was flat against what the Rule allowed for cloistered nuns. But Domina Alys had been on the edge of agreeing to it, encouraged by the eager nodding of most of the nuns to Sister Amicia's words, until Frevisse had stood up and pointed out the impropriety of their going out for no better reason than their amusement. She knew afterwards that she had been less diplomatic than she might have been, and very likely Domina Alys would have overborn the objection in the high-handed way she favoured in settling any problem, but Sister Thomasine had also, very uncharacteristically, risen to her feet and in her soft but, on this occasion at least, definite voice said that, let the rest of them do as they would, she would never, not now or any other time, God keep her soul, go with them into such sin. Then, having not given a challenge but merely stated what she felt, she had sat down again, eyes lowered, hands folded in her lap, as inward-drawn and meek as usual. What the others did was now their own concern. But so pale, frail, unworldly it was hard to imagine she had ever lived outside the nunnery, she was thought among the nuns to be a saint in the making, and her words, rather than Frevisse's protest, had given Domina Alys pause, so that her eventual, grudging decision had been that for today at least there would be no unseemly going abroad.

But what could be forgiven – or at least ignored – from Sister Thomasine remained an offence from Frevisse. She had felt the blunt edge of the prioress's displeasure through the day and knew, from past experience, that when Domina Alys had had time to think of something sufficient, she would be paid back fully for her temerity in so overtly interfering.

But how could she not when such a wrong was about to be done? Irritable with helplessness, she repeated, 'What can we do?'

'Keep quiet?' Dame Claire asked.

'How can I? How can you?'

'I don't know. But have you thought that maybe the problem doesn't completely lie with her?'

'No, I hadn't thought that.'

'She feels we disturb her rule by doubting her.'

'Her rule is something to be doubted.'

'She's done the priory some good, you know.'

Frevisse intensely disliked it when Dame Claire insisted on seeing the other side of a matter whose nearer side offended Frevisse so greatly. But Dame Claire was right. Through Domina Alys's influence with her large family, St Frideswide's now had two novices, which was two more novices than the priory had had in five years. Besides, her family, pleased with her new position, had given the priory a goodly gift of money on Lady Day and talk was lively on how it should be used, with feelings running strongly several ways but mainly pleasure in the fact that there was spare money to be talked of at all.

So, yes, Domina Alys had done the priory some good. 'But—'

'And she's right in feeling that we – you and I – disturb her rule.'

'We don't do anything beyond sometimes question what she does,' Frevisse protested. 'You can't say I was wrong this morning.'

'No. Nor yesterday when you asked why she meant to rent the Northampton messuage to her cousin at a lesser rate than we had been receiving for it.'

'It was a needed question. Someone had to ask it.'

'Undoubtedly. But it was you who did.'

'Because no one else dared.'

'Exactly.'

Dame Claire looked sideways up at Frevisse to see if she had taken the point. After a moment, Frevisse smiled wryly in return. 'And it doesn't help that I don't always question her in the mildest way possible.'

'Nor does it help that you do it so often.'

Frevisse made a small gesture of helplessness, and Dame Claire said, 'I know. You tend to see matters more clearly than most do, and for good measure you think about them, and then, beyond that, you have the courage – more courage than I have – to speak out when you think you should.'

'The courage or the stupidity.'

'That, too, upon occasion,' Dame Claire agreed equitably. 'But whether you speak out or not, she assumes that you disapprove of whatever she does, and sometimes the look on your face shows all too clearly that you do. I, on the other hand, annoy her simply by being here at all.'

And that, Frevisse knew, was true enough too. Dame Claire's mere presence was reminder of what everyone knew Domina

Edith had intended for the priory; and so to Domina Alys's choleric mind, Dame Claire's presence was an ongoing rebuke.

'And it doesn't help,' Frevisse said, 'that we keep each other company at recreation time.'

'It makes her more suspicious of both of us,' Dame Claire agreed.

'I'll try to bridle my tongue. That may eventually help.'

Dame Claire did not answer. Their walking had brought them back to the bottom of the garden, a little way from where Sister Thomasine still stood, her face lifted to the thrush still singing in the pear tree. By unspoken accord, they both stopped to listen, too, though Frevisse's mind stayed more on what they had been saying than on the beauty of the evening. And so did Dame Claire's, apparently, for shortly she said, quite quietly, 'I have an idea that might help.'

Frevisse gave a small sideways movement of her head to show she was listening without looking away from the bird above them. Dame Claire went on, 'I'm going to confess in chapter that I've been guilty of proud and sinful thoughts and of failure to keep a vow.' She slightly raised her hand to stop Frevisse's startled, disbelieving response. 'Last year I was so afraid Domina Edith would have pain in her dying and that there would be nothing I could do for it that I vowed to St Frideswide that if she would give her a quiet death, free from pain, I'd make a pilgrimage on foot to her shrine in Oxford.'

'Dame Claire!' Frevisse said in distress. A nun was not supposed to make vows beyond the limits of her obedience to her prioress, vows she could not possibly keep without her prioress's permission.

'I know. But I thought then, God forgive me' – she crossed herself – 'that I would be prioress after her so there was no problem. I simply wanted her to die peacefully. I never imagined I would have to ask Dame Alys's permission to keep the vow. So I've added to my sin by waiting this long to ask it.'

'And you'd tell all that in chapter? In front of everyone?' She did not add, though it was the strongest thought she had: to Domina Alys's face?

'It's the only way. It will clear my soul and give her enough satisfaction at my humiliation she may no longer feel I'm such a threat to her.'

'But do you think she'll actually give you leave? She could simply release you from the vow and give you heavy penance here.'

'I think to have me out of here a while – and to show how generous-spirited she is – she'll give me leave. I'm nearly sure of it. But I want you to be the one who goes with me.'

No nun could go abroad beyond the nunnery walls alone. At very least another nun had to keep her company, and Frevisse immediately grasped what Dame Claire was asking of her.

'You want that I should make confession in chapter, too, when you do. Of my prideful thoughts against her. And ask to be sent on foot with you, for my penance.'

'Yes.'

Frevisse stared at the ground in front of her without seeing it. 'It won't work,' she said. 'She'll never allow it.'

'She will,' Sister Thomasine said. Her voice despite its softness startled them; they had forgotten she was there. She turned to face them. 'She'll gladly let you go if you give her the chance.'

'How do you know?' Dame Claire asked gently. Unlike Frevisse for whom patience with Sister Thomasine was too often an effort, Dame Claire was always willing to listen to her.

Sister Thomasine tilted her head a little, as if she found the question puzzling. 'She will. That's all.'

The sunset was far faded toward darkness, and Sister Thomasine's face was only a pale blur within the circle of her white wimple, its expression unreadable, but her voice in all its gentleness was completely assured, beyond any question of might be or maybe. Frevisse shivered and told herself that it was only from the chill that was creeping in now the last of the light was going. She turned to Dame Claire and said with more firmness of purpose than she felt, 'I'll do it, and God have mercy on us,' and was glad that the cloister bell began to ring then, calling them in to Compline and putting an end to any chance of further talk.

Chapter 3

STRETCHED OUT ON his back on the sun-warmed grassy bank, his hands under his head and all at ease, Giles watched the oak leaves lightly moving on the branches high between him and the clear sky. Around him the easy talk of folk met by chance on the road went quietly on without need for him to listen to its pointlessness. Since they would easily be at Minster Lovell before nightfall no one was making any haste over their midday meal here in the oak's wide shade on the grassy verge of the road. The weather had held mostly dry and warm these past few days of their journeying so they could afford this sort of leisure along the way. Giles supposed that was something to be thankful for, even if there was not much else.

They had already been to Winchcombe Abbey and three of the other Kenelm churches. And Winchcombe at least had been tolerable. Barely. The abbey's purpose might be holy – though the monks were making a pretty penny off their saint, vows of poverty notwithstanding – but the town grown up outside the abbey gates had more worldly pleasures to offer those who, like Giles, had something other than prayers in mind. But the rest of the Kenelm shrines were proving to be paltry places, scattered long thwart and thitherward around the countryside in one-street villages miles from anywhere worth being, with inns not worth the name or food worth the eating. And now there was the company Lionel was choosing to keep.

They had set out from Knyvet with eleven in their company: he and Edeyn and Lionel, no trouble there, and seven servants to see to them and the horses and the baggage, and Martyn of course, damn him. A manageable lot, but leave it to Lionel to take up along the way with a handful of chance-met strangers, none of them worth the bother to spit on. The franklin alone with his great gut-laugh was enough to hold against Lionel until doomsday, and they had only been in his company since mid-morning. The man claimed to be bound on business somewhere but was in no apparent haste about it, willing to amble the day away with them and now lingering over his wayside dinner with the rest. By his own boast – and, God, could the man boast – he had been as far as Exeter to the south, Worcester to the west, and Oxford to the east, and seemed to think that meant he had seen the world. So far as Giles was concerned, the very set of his regrettable hat proclaimed him a lout-wit.

And then there were the graceless, ham-handed pair of yeomen they had come on yesterday, likewise pilgrimaging to St Kenelm at Minster Lovell so Lionel had taken up with them on the instant, the fool. A father and son and plainly more used to following their heavy-hocked bay geldings behind a plough than riding them. Roughly dressed and coarsely mannered and so cross-eyed it sure as damnation must bring ill-luck to look them in the face, they had kept suitably silent at first, but Lionel had drawn them out with questions and the father had spent yester evening at the inn going on at length about the problems there were in ploughing when the fields were too wet. As if anyone else here cared so long as it was done when it was supposed to be done and no trouble made about it.

If Lionel did not bother to bestir the lot of them soon, they might not make it to Minster Lovell by suppertime after all, and Giles was vastly looking forward to Minster Lovell, if only so he could shut a few doors between himself and these nattering fools. And now, God help him, they were trying to do riddles!

Without enough wit among the franklin and clod-pated father and son to tell them to go in when it rained, Lionel was trying to do riddles with them, to see if they had any new ones! As if there weren't enough old ones to send Giles out of his mind.

He rolled his head slightly to the side to look at Edeyn's profile where she sat beside him, and past her to Lionel. They were all grouped in a lop-sided circle on cushions on the grass, with only himself drawn a little apart with a vague thought after they had finished eating that he might drowse the time away until they moved on. Their talk and laughter had cost him hope of being rid of them even that long, and now he reached out an apparently idle hand to take hold of Edeyn's where it lay on the grass between them and fondled it. She glanced around at him with a smile. He smiled back, aware that across from her Lionel was watching.

Watch on, old Lionel, and see what you can never have, Giles thought. He raised Edeyn's hand to his lips and kissed it lingeringly. Edeyn looked around at him again, her smile deepening with pleasure, her face lightly colouring with embarrassment. Giles enjoyed that in her – her stupid modesty that made her shy of showing what she was, her wantonness when he could have her alone in bed for long enough to rouse her.

There was wantonness in every woman. Some needed longer to have it dragged out of them than others did but it was there. Because with Edeyn there had been time, he had made a long and pleasurable process, after his lusting for her had been slaked, of first finding hers and then waking her fully to it. Now occasionally for extra pleasure, he let Lionel see it, too. There was a certain look that Lionel had – a way his gaze slid away when Giles handled Edeyn in front of him – that made the moment, the possession, more pleasurable by far. Lionel might plague him with these fools just now, but he could plague Lionel any time he chose, simply by reminding him whose Edeyn was and what Giles could do with her whenever he wanted to.

It did not change the fact that Giles had to listen to this drivel now but it evened out the suffering a little.

And wonder of wonders, the fat franklin was coming out with another riddle so old it was wrinkled.

'I think it was my aunt told it to me when I was a lad. I've always favoured it. She was as clever a woman as I've ever known. It goes this way. A houseful, a holeful, but no one can gather a bowlful. Eh?'

Lionel and Martyn held back admirably. It was the cross-eyed yeoman father who exclaimed, after a moment's hard remembering because even he had heard that one before, 'Smoke!' At Lionel's praise – Lionel would praise a cloud for raining, he was that soft – the oaf grinned but then realized, appalled, that it was now his turn to find a riddle, and one he remembered the answer to, too, which would make it doubly hard, Giles supposed. The dolt was hesitating mightily before his son leaned over and whispered something to him, making him brighten. 'Aye. There's one,' he said with relief. 'How can an apple be without any core?'

Oh God! Giles dropped his head back down on the cushion under it and said toward the sky with undisguised disgust, 'When it's a blossom, damn it. That one's older than the smoke one. Even Edeyn knows it.'

'Giles!' Lionel snapped. 'You have a way—' He cut himself off from whatever angry thing he had been about to say.

Good old Lionel. Not even allowing himself some temper. Why didn't he do everyone a favour and die since he wanted so much to be a saint?

With an unwarranted enthusiasm that showed he was glad of the diversion, the franklin exclaimed, 'Well, and what's this coming then?'

Willing to be diverted by almost anything, Giles rolled his head sideways and saw that the lot of them were looking away along the road and Lionel was rising to his feet. Good. Maybe whatever it was would set them all on their way again. Giles sat up.

He nearly lay down again. There had been no other travellers today and what was it now but a pair of nuns. There was a lack of excitement for you.

Still, they were on foot. There was a priest and a servant riding attendance behind them so they were not out wayward and wandering, but the reasons two nuns would be travelling a-foot were few, and penance came to mind immediately. If that was it, they must have made serious offence to have been sent out like this.

Or one of them had offended and the other was sent along to keep her company, no nun allowed to go alone outside her cloister.

Giles's speculation veered toward the lewd. This could be interesting after all. But a clearer look killed his hopes. In those obscuring habits, with wimples tight around their faces, a nun's age could be hard to judge, but he could tell enough here to guess that whatever these two had done, it had not been out of youthful folly. The smaller of the two might have been game-some when she was young – there was the possibility of a shapely body under that crow-black gown yet – but Giles judged the taller one had always been too sharp-featured to be worth a man's bothering with her. Probably they had done nothing worse than talk back to their prioress once too often or maybe slapped another nun when they were quarrelling.

What a waste of women nunhood was.

And now Lionel was sending Martyn forward to ask them to join them in the shade. Oh yes, just what was lacking to make the day more dull – pointless talk with useless women and more delay in being on their way.

Frevisse and Dame Claire stopped where they were and waited while young John Naylor went forward to talk to the man come out from among the travellers under the tree. They looked a prosperous, leisurely group, probably no other than travellers like themselves, but it was always better to be sure and she had come to trust young John's judgement these past few days. He was nephew to the priory's steward and only lately come into service at St Frideswide's. Frevisse suspected that Domina Alys had chosen him as one of their companions because he was young and likely to be too inexperienced to be much use on the way, but Domina Alys had been wrong in that. Young John was as longheaded and steady as his uncle despite his youth.

Not that Domina Alys probably much cared one way or other, now that she had them actually out of her way. She had agreed readily to the idea of Dame Claire's penance, just as Thomasine had said she would, and added to it confession in front of the whole house and a few nights spent in penitential prayer in the church before they actually set out. She had accepted the idea of Frevisse going with her with equal ease, and made further advantage for herself by appointing Father Henry, the priory's priest, as their other companion, giving her chance to bring in, even if only temporarily, one of her nephews as priory priest in his place.

She had probably thought that Father Henry would be as little use as young John Naylor along the way, since he was not among the quick of wit, and in that she had been more right than about young John; but Father Henry was a good-humoured traveller and that counted for much when travelling together so long and slowly as they were going.

And it was slowly. Frevisse had spent much of her girlhood on the roads with her parents through England, France, the Low Countries, and even once to St James in Spain. The troubles, habits, and joys of journeying were almost as much a part of her as praying was, and the ways of it came back to her readily whenever there was chance, few and far between as chances had been since she had entered St Fridewide's. She expected this small jaunt to give her no particular trouble of mind or body, but it was different with Dame Claire. Her upbringing had been more gentle than Frevisse's and she had begun to suffer toward the end of their first day on the road, and suffered worse the next morning when her muscles had had time to stiffen and her feet to swell. But she had her resources, too. The Benedictine Rule required the priory to give shelter and care to travellers, and she had come to know something of the needs of folk afoot and had thought to bring along an ointment that eased soreness when deeply rubbed in on legs and feet. That had helped yesterday, and today had gone fairly well once Dame Claire's early morning's stiffness had worn off, though their pace was still slower than Frevisse would have set for herself or in greater need.

But there was no need for hurry. Dame Claire's penance was as much in the journey as in anything and there was no set day for their return, though that could be trouble as well as benefit. As Dame Claire had pointed out in their first morning on the road, 'If we make haste and come back in too short a while, I'll be told I scanted my penance. But if we take too long at it, I'll be held to have been dawdling, frivolous with my time.'

'So we had best do simply what feels right as we go along,' Frevisse had said. 'Then our consciences will be clear, no matter what she says of us.' Because they were never going to satisfy Domina Alys, no matter what they did or how they did it. And if they were 'too long' about it, let Domina Alys take some of the blame herself. It was her doing that they were going well aside from their way, to Minster Lovell instead of straight to Oxford.

To fulfill her vow, Dame Claire was supposed to walk the some thirty miles from the priory to St Frideswide's great monastery and shrine in Oxford town, there confess and receive absolution from the prior himself for her sins of pride and contumely against her prioress, and then pray at the shrine before returning home. But there was presently a property trouble in Priors Byfield, the village near the nunnery. Some of it was owned by the nunnery, some by Lord Lovell, and some of it was freehold. The nunnery and Lord Lovell's stewards were usually able to resolve between themselves problems that arose but there was a matter to hand now that the two men were not agreeing on as fast as Domina Alys was willing to tolerate, so she had decided to send copies of what she thought were the relevant documents directly to Lord Lovell. That way he could see what a fool his man was being and decide in the nunnery's favour. But messengers cost money, and since she had two nuns bound more or less in Lord Lovell's direction, why pay the cost of a messenger when her nuns could do the task instead?

Frevisse's uncharitable thought had been that Domina Alys would receive double value for her choice because it would also keep her and Dame Claire that much longer away and give them that much further to walk.

She would have to confess and do penance for that thought against her prioress, but she did not much care. Away from Domina Alys was exactly where she wanted to be, and the longer away the better. Besides, the journey so far had been pleasurable, the April days warm under lightly clouded skies, the roads dry, with spring birdsong and early flowers along the way and reasonably comfortable places to sleep at night. It was fortunate this was not supposed to be a pilgrimage of penance for her at least; she was finding far too much in it to enjoy, including being away from her prioress.

But she was also ready to stop for their midday meal and rest and prayers, and sight of the tall oak's top ahead of them had promised a goodly place for all of that. It had been a disappointment to find its shade already in use, and the best they could hope for now was, first, to be invited to share it and then that the travellers would shortly go on and leave them.

Young John returned, to bow and say, 'It's a Lionel Knyvet and his folk and some others travelling with them. You're asked to join them if you'd like.'

'What did you think of them?' Dame Claire asked.

'The man was mannerly. I think it would be right enough if you wish it. They seem honest.'

Frevisse held back from saying, And it's not as if we had much to offer thieves anyway. The nunnery's imposed rule of silence had helped her learn to curb her tongue through the years but not always her thoughts, and she was finding now that she was away from the strong hold she had kept on them under Domina Alys's sway, just how impatient and caustic they tended to be anymore, even when there was no present cause.

Dame Claire was asking her with a look if they should accept the invitation. It was clear she was ready to, and behind them Father Henry, always ready for the chance of new talk with strangers, had nudged his horse closer to hear their choice. There was no real reason to decline so Frevisse nodded agreement.

They were a mixed company. Aside from the servants, there were six men and a woman; but two of the men were clearly yeomen or less, and it was not the oldest of the other men who came to welcome Frevisse, Dame Claire and Father Henry when they had dismounted but one of the considerably younger men.

He introduced himself with a slight bow and courteous smile. 'My ladies, good sir. I'm Lionel Knyvet. My thanks for your joining us this while.'

He was somewhere in his twenties, Frevisse guessed. Tall and not particularly well featured, with long bones and a large jaw. His heavy-lidded eyes made him look as if he were too much given to sleep, but there was an old scar white across his forehead and bridge of his nose as if he had had adventures when he was younger. He had given no title so he was not noble, but the rich cloth and good cut of his clothing and the way he travelled in company and with servants and packhorses showed he was well born. Or at least wealthy. And his manners could not have been better.

'Your man said you're bound for Minster Lovell and so are we.'

He included the others behind him with a movement of his hand. 'Would you care to join us the few miles more there are to go?'

'That's kind of you,' Dame Claire said, 'and surely your company would be welcome, but I fear we would slow you over-much, going on foot as we do.'

'A vow?' he asked.

'A vow,' Dame Claire agreed.

Lionel Knyvet accepted that without more question. 'Then give me the pleasure of sharing our food?'

'We'll be grateful for the shade and sitting with you, surely,' Dame Claire said. 'But we have food of our own and no need to trouble you.'

'Not trouble but pleasure, my lady. Pray you, let me do you that courtesy.'

His own courtesy was so great, it would have been discourteous to refuse him. Dame Claire smiled. 'We'd be pleased of your kindness. Thank you.'

John Naylor had gone aside with the horses to where the others' mounts were grazing slack-girthed along the hedge. He would join the Knyvet servants for his meal, but Dame Claire, Frevisse, and Father Henry went with Master Knyvet and were introduced to the others, the only woman among them first. 'My cousin's wife, Mistress Knyvet.'

She was very young, not far out of girlhood. Prettiness and health bloomed in her face, unmarred yet by any of life's heaviness. But for all her prettiness and youth, she was sensibly dressed for travel in a close-sleeved brown linen gown, with a simple white wimple and veil to protect her hair and neck from dust and sun, and she made them a pleasant, smiling curtsy.

'My cousin Giles,' Lionel said.

The family resemblance to Lionel was strongly there in his colouring and face, but his better-proportioned, unscarred features were far closer to handsome than Lionel's had ever been. He bowed curtly, not bothering to hide his lack of enthusiasm at the introduction, said perfunctorily, 'Sir. My ladies,' and sat down again.

Gesturing to the cushions where she had been seated herself, his wife said with far more grace, 'Pray you, sit here.' And when Frevisse and Dame Claire gratefully had and she had joined them, Lionel introduced the rest of the company. First the older man. 'Master Bernard Geffers, keeping us company this while.'

'A franklin from near Chipping Norton,' Master Geffers added by way of further explanation. 'Both pleased and honoured to meet you thus.'

Frevisse's immediate thought was that she did not like his hat. The style he had set for it, with its hood pulled up on top of his head into a coxcomb and its liripipe wrapped around to hold it in place, was much too young a fashion for his years. And so was the flourish he gave to his bow before he likewise sat down and edged a little closer, as if anticipating a good talk as soon as there was chance.

'And Hamon and Will Stenby, on pilgrimage like us to St Kenelm's at Minster Lovell,' Lionel said.

Except in age, the two men were so alike to look at that Frevisse readily guessed them to be father and son, the elder somewhat more stooped across his wide shoulders, the younger more firmly fleshed under his tan. They each had an eye crossed toward their nose, the father's left one, the son's right, making even their most solemn expressions amusing. Their plain, dun-coloured, knee-length pilgrim tunics had seen other journeys, though not on them, Frevisse guessed, judging by the ill-fit and the Stenbys' awkward bows that told how unused they were to meeting strangers. They had probably never been more than a handful of miles from their village until now, and she wondered what vow or penance had set them on their way.

'And Martyn Gravesend,' Lionel said.

The last man took half a step forward and bowed. He was the man who had come to greet them on the road, and by his quiet garb of doublet and hose and riding boots he was a servant, so that Frevisse was disconcerted by the introduction. There had been no thought of introducing young John Naylor to anyone. 'My steward,' Lionel said.

Frevisse hoped she hid her reaction. But though Martyn Gravesend's bow had been simply what it should have been, neither falsely humble nor over-bold, simply assured and with no pretension to more than he was, the slightest quirk at one corner of his mouth as he stepped back from it told he was neither so grave as his name nor at all unused to Lionel's impropriety and people's reaction to it.

Dame Claire and Frevisse made small, stiff movements of their heads to him, acknowledging the introduction as barely as they might. Father Henry hesitated to do even that much, and the moment was saved from further awkwardness by Mistress Knyvet asking, 'You've walked far today?'

'However many miles it's been since dawn,' Dame Claire said. 'And for two days before then.'

The talk went around to where everyone had come from and where they were going, until a servant brought bread trenchers laid with cheese and cold meat and even a hard boiled egg.

'I hope this suits, my ladies, sir,' Mistress Knyvet said.

'Very well,' Dame Claire assured her. 'My deep thanks.' Frevisse and Father Henry echoed her while another servant poured wine for everyone.

They were all seated now, except for Martyn Gravesend who stood a little behind Lionel's left shoulder, where he should be but occasionally included by Lionel in the conversation.

Now Dame Claire was saying to Lionel, 'You're kind to do so much for us. You were readying to leave when we came, I think?'

'Thinking of it, no more,' Lionel lightly answered. 'The day's too fine to waste in haste.'

'And it's not so many miles to Minster Lovell that we need worry,' Mistress Knyvet added.

'But weather is always a chancy thing, no matter what it looks like just now,' her husband said. 'And night falls on even the most pleasant day.'

'It would take a miracle to make rain fall from this clear of a sky,' Lionel said.

Giles shrugged without answer to that. His wife held out the goblet they shared to him with a smile that was either commiseration or appeasement. Frevisse had already decided he was a tense-tempered man and wished Mistress Knyvet luck.

Master Geffers began recalling a particularly rain-fouled journey he had once made to Gloucester town. Father Henry ventured an opinion that such good weather as at present meant the harvest might be good this year. The Stenby father and son quickly took up that thought, agreeing that they hoped so.

The conversation lagged a little then, weather and travel having been covered with some degree of thoroughness, but Dame Claire, Father Henry and Frevisse were still finishing their meal so that no one could take the moment to suggest they should all be on their way. It was Mistress Knyvet who smiled and asked, 'Martyn, have you any new riddles?'

The steward smiled back. 'I do, as it happens.'

Lionel half-turned on his cushion to look up at him, his face alight with laughter. 'You've been holding out on me? Unfair.'

'If I emptied out all that's in my head ...' Martyn started.

'... there'd be a puddle on the ground,' Giles finished.

Master Geffers caught the beginning of a laugh behind his hand. Lionel turned an angry look on Giles and might have spoken, but Mistress Knyvet, hurriedly passing the goblet to her husband again, glanced aside at him, and Lionel held back what he might have said and turned again to Martyn who had not changed colour or expression. He might not have heard Giles at all, except he did not finish his sentence but said, 'Try this. In a garden was laid a pretty fair maid, as fair as the light of the morn. The first day of her life she was made a wife, and she died ere she was born.'

Giles, done with the goblet, yawned his boredom and lay back on a cushion behind him. The Stenbys and Father Henry looked utterly lost but the rest of them set to the problem, Lionel with open delight. Dame Claire repeated, thinking about it, 'And died ere she was born?' Her literal mind that served her so well as infirmarian was a liability when it came to riddles, and no one else seemed to be faring any better. Only Frevisse, given to thinking aside from other people's usual ways even at the best of times, suddenly saw the way of it and declared, 'It's Eve of course! She was made from Adam's rib and never born at all.'

Martyn declared, 'You have it!' Lionel laughed and clapped his hands in admiration. Everyone else groaned or continued to look bewildered.

'Now you have to ask one,' Lionel declared. 'Make it hard. She'll match you, Martyn, and serve you right. You've had your own way at this too long.'

'You're jealous because you can't keep a riddle in your head long enough to bring it to me and ask it,' Martyn returned in kind.

'And I swear you've cheated by sending to London for a riddle book and kept it secret. That's how you manage to look so clever,' Lionel shot back.

'And you wish you'd thought of it first,' Martyn returned.

That was bold, between servant and master, but Lionel only laughed. Frevisse wondered how it went in the Knyvet household with them more like to friends than master and steward; but she had her riddle and said before they could go on, 'A shoemaker made shoes of no leather but all the elements taken together – earth, water, fire, and air – and every customer had two pair.'

'Ah!' Lionel cried. 'Martyn, where's your book? I've heard that one and can't remember it!'

Dame Claire murmured, 'A shoemaker? "Earth, water, fire, and air"?'

Away along the hedge one of the horses stamped at a fly, his hoof thudding softly against the turf. Martyn Gravesend's expression changed, betraying he suddenly had the answer, but Mistess Knyvet cried out before he could, 'Horsehoes! It's horseshoes, isn't it?'

'Yes, horseshoes,' Frevisse agreed.

Pleased beyond measure, Mistress Knyvet exclaimed, 'Lionel, I finally guessed one! All on my own!'

Lionel and Martyn were both laughing at her, as pleased as she was, and Lionel reached out to take and squeeze her hand. 'Haven't I told you that all you need to do is think crookedly, like Martyn does, and you could do it?'

Mistress Knyvet's delight shifted to dismay. 'But now I have to have a riddle. Giles, can you think of one for me?'

Her husband had occasionally watched what was going on through half-opened eyes, but now to his wife's plea, he only shook his head and closed his eyes completely.

'Giles!' she pleaded.

'The cat one from the other day,' he said.

'But that's no good! Lionel and Martyn already know it!'

'Then tell them they can't guess.'

Lionel rescued her with, 'What we should do is not be guessing anything but being on our way.'

Dame Claire, Father Henry, and Frevisse had finished eating, and he was undeniably right. It was time they were all about their business again.

'But we'll all meet at Minster Lovell,' Lionel added, 'and that will be pleasant.'

Servants gathered up the cushions to pack away in a pannier on one of the horses. Girths were tightened and horses brought while the men talked of how far it might yet be and Dame Claire made light conversation with Mistress Knyvet on the beautiful day, Frevisse with them but not interested. Giles, already mounted, said impatiently, 'Edeyn, come on. You delay us all.'

Since he was the only one so far mounted, Frevisse thought his comment made him look a fool; but his wife's expression was shaded somewhere between alarm at his overt displeasure and resentment at his tone before she smoothed it away, excused herself, and went to her horse, leaving Frevisse appreciative of the fact that though it was difficult for her to be worthy of her own godly bridegroom Christ, she was spared the awkward temper of a mortal husband.

The others were mounting now. Farewells were made and the riders gathered on the road, Father Henry and young John waiting aside with their horses. The Stenbys' two sturdy bays each had a scarlet ribbon frivolously braided into their forelock by someone who hoped their venture into the world beyond their village would be gay as well as holy, and for no good reason Frevisse's spirits rose a little at the sight. She had not known how uncheerful and unsociable she was until they had joined this mostly happy group. She must think more of scarlet ribbons and less of Domina Alys.

She and Dame Claire stood side by side to watch the Knyvets and the others go, waving just before they were lost to sight around the next curve of the road. Alone again, they knelt where they were beside the road, joined by Father Henry to say the prayers of None together. John Naylor stayed with the horses but bowed his head with the quiet willingness to prayer that had helped make his companionship acceptable these past few days. It probably helped that he was spared the full complexity and length of the offices' psalms and prayers, but Frevisse was pleased that, even shortened, None's prayers still included, *Pes enim meus stetit in via recta*. My foot truly keeps on the right way. A line most apt for travellers, even with so few miles now between them and Minster Lovell.

Chapter 4

I N THE WARM light of late afternoon their way brought them down into a soft curve of valley where a narrow river ran glittering in the sun between low banks. Happily this was one they did not have to cross; the road turned to run along it toward a stretch of houses with the squat tower of a church at their far end and a glimpse of taller buildings beyond it so that Frevisse guessed their day's walking was nearly done.

The road became a street between the timbered houses. The smells of cooking came from the open doorways, and a cluster of small children pulled back cheerfully from their game in the middle of the street to watch them pass. When Frevisse and Dame Claire smiled at them, they smiled back, a happy, barefoot, untidy little group, dirty with their day's play but well kept under it.

A woman came out on the house doorstep nearest them. One of the little girls ran to her and caught hold of her skirts, not frighted, merely asserting her claim, and the woman laid a hand on her head in absent caress while taking in the sight of the four travellers. She smiled when Dame Claire asked, 'Is this Minster Lovell?' and answered with a curtsy, 'Indeed, my lady.'

'And the manor house?' Dame Claire asked.

Other housewives were coming to their doorsteps, drawn first by their children's silence and now by the chance to look at strangers. Pleased to be the one speaking to them, the woman pointed on along the street. 'There beyond the church. Just go on the way you're going. You're nearly there.'

Dame Claire gave their thanks and a blessing that the woman gladly curtsied again to receive.

Past the houses, the road left river as well as village behind to skirt a low churchyard wall. Some of the church's stonework was new and the yard was neatly kept around the grave markers, the paths lately gravelled. Frevisse noted it all the way she had noted the quiet prosperity of the village, but what she noted more was the wall at the churchyard's east end. It was higher than a mounted man could see over and plastered a shining, unweathered white. It was safe guess that Minster Lovell manor house, the end of their day's walking, and the chance of a good night's rest were beyond it.

The horses jinked their harness, pulling at their reins, sensing along with their riders that they were nearing travel's end for the day and wanting to quicken pace. Frevisse had the same urge, but Dame Claire was past going any faster so she held herself back the way Father Henry and young John were holding back their horses. They would all of them arrive no sooner than the slowest of them and that, in God's will, would be soon enough.

Beyond the churchyard, the road went on along the wall, now taller than a rider's head, and when the wall turned to the right, the road went with it. On their left now there were barns and byres and the sounds of men and animals about their business at day's end. On their right, above the wall, red-tiled roofs showed and two chimneys whose smoke was hopefully from kitchens, and then at last there was the gateway, its gates open, showing that the way ran as a cobbled, covered passageway through the thickness of buildings built inside and above the wall, into the manor yard.

She, Dame Claire, and Father Henry paused to let John Naylor go ahead of them. He spoke briefly to the man who sauntered out from the gateway shadows and then turned and nodded for them to follow him on through.

The wide yard was full of sunlight and edged by late afternoon shadows. Its south side, to their left, ran along the river with a plain wall and a small gateway standing open to the river. The other three sides were enclosed with long ranges of stone buildings. Low on either side of the gateway, at the north end of the yard they rose to a high roof of a great hall, while across from the gateway whatever was to be there was still a jumble of builders' scaffolding, partial walls, and piled stone. The workmen were just coming down from their half-built walls, powdered with stone dust, laughing and loud among themselves. Other folk were going and coming from here to there and otherwise across the yard, busy with purposes that had nothing to do with the new-come travellers.

Frevisse had a disconcerting moment of longing for the familiarity of St Frideswide's, where everyone and their duties, including her own, were known. Here she was only a stranger, and her only purpose in being here at all was to deliver a document, a thing any servant could have done.

While she was still sorting out her feelings, putting them out of her way, a pair of stablehands came to take the horses. As they led them off, a servant came toward them from the hall, a hand raised to draw their attention and in greeting. He was an older man, dressed in plain livery of good blue cloth, with Lord Lovell's badge of a hunting dog on his left breast. 'From St Frideswide's?' he asked, as if already sure of his answer. Dame Claire agreed that they were and he went on, 'We were told you were coming. My lady set me to watch for you. If you'll please to come with me?'

They readily would, thankful that Lionel Knyvet must have spoken of them and brought them this welcome. The man led them slantwise across a corner of the yard toward the great hall, to a low-arched doorway that led into a passage. On their right, to judge by the good odours and bustle beyond the doorways there, was the kitchen. On their left, halfway along the wooden screen, a single wide doorway led into the great hall itself and Frevisse supposed that was the way they were to go, but, as they reached it, a girl too well gowned to be a servant came toward them from the far end of the passage, calling gaily, 'Have you found them, Hugh? How very good of you.'

Frevisse held back the urge to say it had not been hard for him, once they had walked in through the gateway, but that was discourteous, her tiredness speaking, not her manners.

'I'm Luce,' the girl said with a bobbing curtsy to Dame Claire, Frevisse, and Father Henry. 'One of Lady Lovell's ladies.' She was softly pretty in a way that would likely go to plump soon, sure and pleasant in her manners, bright with cheerfulness. 'Lady Lovell thought you might want to wash and rest a little first. I'm to see you to your room and then to Lady Lovell, if you like. Oh, Sire Benedict!' she said happily to a priest come into the passageway from the hall. 'They're here. See?'

Unless he's blind, he does, Frevisse thought.

Luce turned her smile back on them. 'Sire Benedict is our priest. My lady thought he and yours could spend their time together.'

Sire Benedict bowed gravely to them and then to Father Henry. He was an older man, cleanly kept in his black priest's gown, his tonsure fresh and smooth. He looked more slight than he actually was next to Father Henry's great size, and Father Henry was more rumpled than ever next to him, his tonsure as usual nearly hidden by his thick, wilfully curling yellow hair. But they said polite things to each other and went away together while Luce said, 'And Hugh will see to your man.'

She dismissed young John with a smiling nod and gathered Frevisse and Dame Claire after her with an out-held arm, heading them the way the priests had gone, into the hall.

It was new-built as so much of Minster Lovell seemed to be, bright-plastered, no wear even to the stone threshold. It opened up around them, high and wide but overly tall for its rather modest length. Frevisse had to resist the urge to crane her head back to stare up at the high rafters, but she saw the sense of the disproportion; instead of a fireplace neatly set into a wall, as was the fashion now, the hall's hearth lay in the hall's centre with nowhere for the smoke to go except up to the ceiling among the rafters. There were openings in each gable end for a cross-draught to carry it away, but how odd that Lord Lovell had made his manor over new and yet kept an open hearth at its heart.

There was only a scattering of folk about, servants who noticed them but did not stare. The late afternoon flurry of work to set the tables up for supper had not started yet. Luce talked busily of how the Knyvets had come a few hours ago – 'And of course Lady Lovell wished to see Edeyn again as soon as might be, and Edeyn said you were coming, that's how we knew' – as she led them the length of the hall and up on the low dais where the lord and his family would dine, raised slightly above the lesser folk. There were doors at either end of it. Father Henry was just disappearing after Sire Benedict through the rightward one, and Luce said, waving cheerily after them, 'They'll do well together. Sire Benedict is a friendly sort, though he doesn't look it,' as she took Frevisse and Dame Claire to the leftward door. It led into a small room with a door to whatever lay beyond the great hall and a spiral stairway going up. They went up, passed another door, and came out into a long room generously windowed at each end and comfortably, richly furnished. The solar, Frevisse guessed, where the family could withdraw from the more general, crowded life of the great hall when they chose.

'Our room is just through here,' Luce said, heading for another doorway across the solar. 'The ladies' chamber. And my lord and lady's is beyond. We'll have other rooms in the north range when it's done and all this will be my lord and lady's chambers, but for now, with the building and all, we're terribly together. I hope you don't mind being crowded in to sleep with all of us.'

The ladies' chamber was an airy room, with a line of mullioned windows overlooking the yard and a clutter of women's things around the beds and chests and benches along its inner wall. Nearest the door a bed and the space around it had been tidied and cleared, with a wide basin and a cloth-covered ewer set on the bench at its foot. Luce held out her hand to show this was for them. 'There's warmed water in the ewer. At least it's supposed to be warm.' Luce touched the ewer. 'Yes, that's all right then. And someone will have your baggage here soon. Is there anything else you need?'

'No, I think not,' Dame Claire answered. 'Our thanks. This is very well indeed.'

And it would be better, Frevisse thought, if they could be left alone to wash their faces and hands and road-dirty feet and sit for a while in peace. As if she had read the thought, Luce said, smiling, 'Then I'll come back when you've had a little time to rest. Lady Lovell hopes you'll be at leisure to come to her before supper,' gave them one of her bobbing curtsies, and left them.

'Finally,' Frevisse said, when the girl was well gone and sat down on the bed she and Dame Claire would share.

'She was very courteous,' Dame Claire murmured. 'It was kind of Lady Lovell to send her to see to us.'

Frevisse stood back up with sudden concern. She had been too involved in her own verging on ill-temper – from tiredness, she knew – to remember that Dame Claire was in worse case than she was. Now she saw that Dame Claire was standing as if she were too tired to remember how to sit and wavering slightly on her feet. Frevisse went to her, took her by the arm to steady her, turned her back to the edge of the bed, and said peremptorily, 'Sit.'

Dame Claire sank down with a heavy sigh that was relief mingled with all the weariness she had been trying not to show. 'Thank you. I didn't know I was this tired.'

'Well, you are, and better you admit it than collapse.'

Dame Claire smiled at Frevisse's tartness. Her hands moved vaguely to remove her veil and confining wimple. Frevisse set down the water ewer she had just picked up and did it for her, careful to put the pins in the veil and fold it neatly before setting it aside. Then she took up the ewer again, poured warm water into the basin, soaked a cloth laid to hand for the purpose, and gave it to Dame Claire, who washed her face and hands with the care she gave to any task but very slowly, as if it needed concentration beyond the ordinary.

Frevisse waited and when she had done, took the cloth and knelt down on the floor, took off Dame Claire's shoes and her stockings, and washed her feet. Dame Claire sighed with pleasure. 'Now I should do as much for you.'

'I'll welcome it some other time,' Frevisse said. 'But just now you are going to lie down and stay down until time for supper.'

'Yes,' Dame Claire agreed. 'I think I am.' She was already sinking back toward the pillow, her eyes closing as if nothing could have kept them open. She seemed to be asleep before she was quite fully down.

Frevisse watched and was satisfied. Rest was exactly what Dame Claire needed, and sleep with it was even better. Their other nights on the road had been spent at an inn and the small house of two chantry priests, and their comfort and well-being had not been particularly seen to at either one. Minster Lovell promised to be a respite Dame Claire much needed, and because of their business from St Frideswide's they could hope to spend at least two nights here, giving her a true rest.

Frevisse doubted she would have borne such unaccustomed effort as Dame Claire had faced these past few days with anything like Dame Claire's forbearance. Her own anger at Domina Alys, still there despite the while since they had left St Frideswide's, would have fuelled her aggravation at every discomfort and inconvenience. The only reason it had not was that she had not felt particularly discomfortable or inconvenienced on the road. She had enjoyed the travelling and expected to go on enjoying it, and even now she was not as tired as she had expected to be but wide awake with awareness of being in a new place of which she wanted to see more.

She had washed her face and hands and feet by the time a liveried servant brought the small leathern travelling chest she and Dame Claire were sharing on the journey. It held their few necessities and a change of clean clothing for each of them, no more, and that was enough. Frevisse changed into her own clean gown. Nuns' habits were as near to identical as possible, but the difference between her height and Dame Claire's meant they had gowns far different in length at least.

She was pinning a fresh veil in place when Luce reappeared. Dame Claire had not stirred since settling, her hands folded neatly over her middle, her face eased into the soft lines of utter sleep. Luce took in Frevisse's readiness and Dame Claire's sleep, put cautionary finger to her smiling lips, and beckoned for Frevisse to follow her out of the room.

They paused in the solar by the southward window that overlooked the courtyard, the gateway, the unfinished west range with its scaffolding, and the river beyond the wall. The workmen were all gone but there was still a come-and-go of other people across the yard, most of them in Lord Lovell's blue livery. Frevisee wondered where young John had been taken.

'My lady has asked if you would care to join her in the pleasaunce for the while before supper,' Luce said. 'You and Dame Claire. But I think she'd rather sleep?'

'Sleep is probably best for her now,' Frevisse said, 'but I'll gladly come.'

Luce led her back down the stairs and through the small room into the great hall, down its length and into the wooden screens passage. There instead of back toward the outer door, they turned left, going along it through a different doorway and into a short, stone-vaulted passage that led to another doorway to outside. Luce chatted as they went, mostly about the exigencies of living in a place being newly built. 'So much dust sometimes, and such a noise when the stone-cutters are at it. And the smell of damp plaster. But it will be so splendid when it's done, I'm almost sorry I'll be gone by then. I'm being married at Michaelmas, you know.'

And how would I know that until now that you've told me? Frevisse almost said, but again recognized it for unjustified ill-temper and merely made a murmured response of no particular meaning. Luce obviously liked to talk and Frevisse supposed it was more courteous simply to let her run on rather than interfere by attempting an actual conversation.

They came out of the cool shadows of the stone-vaulted passage into westering sunlight. Frevisse stopped with an exclamation of pleasure at the garden that lay before her. Enclosed on three sides by high walls – the ones that made the east side of the churchyard and ran along the road by which they had come, Frevisse realized – this garden was far larger than St Frideswide's. Here near the house were formal paths among low-fenced small square beds with plants set jewel-like in each of them, singly or a few together, depending on their rarity and beauty. Beyond them, perhaps halfway down the garden's length, a low ornamental lattice fence marked the beginning of a well-groomed greensward shaded by young birch trees, bordered by brick-sided turf benches, and beyond it a green-arboured walkway closing off all but a glimpse of whatever lay at the garden's further end. Across the greensward, among the delicate birch shadows, on cushions and the turf benches, were scattered a half-dozen women and girls and two men in talk among themselves, with one of the women playing lightly on a lute, its notes running like silver water behind their voices, bright as their gowns and occasional laughter.

Lady Lovell's pleasaunce was indeed well named, and to Frevisse's exclamation, Luce said, 'It's my lady's delight,' her own pleasure in it showing plainly.

She led Frevisse the shortest way along the formal paths to the gateway into the greensward. As they went, Frevisse recognized Lionel Knyvett on one of the turf benches, playing with a medium-size white dog that danced around his feet, put paws up on his knees, and ran to fetch a ball when Lionel tossed it away for her. They both seemed to be enjoying it, and though there were other dogs – all ladies' dogs of small to medium size – among the women, this game of toss and fetch seemed to be theirs alone.

His cousin Giles was sitting on cushions under the young trees near his wife who was sitting beside a woman Frevisse guessed was Lady Lovell, because no matter how casually everyone seemed spread around the greensward, she was somehow the centre of them all. And it was to her Luce went, to curtsy deeply and say, 'My lady, Dame Claire is sleeping but I've brought Dame Frevisse.'

With a graceful lift of her hand, Lady Lovell both thanked and dismissed her to join the other women, then smiled for Frevisse to come forward to her. Frevisse did, with as low a curtsy as Luce had made. Lady Lovell acknowledged it with an inclination of her head and said, 'Pray, sit,' indicating a cushion near her. She was richly dressed in a coral-coloured gown trimmed with dark brown velvet at neck and wrists and hem, the colour and richness setting off the cream-white of her skin, her dark eyes and fine arched brows. Her face's smooth oval was framed by several flowing layers of veil so light and fine it could only be of silk, and her wimple was barely a thin band under her chin, leaving her throat bare. A tracery of light lines around her eyes said she was not perfectly young, but Frevisse guessed she was hardly thirty.

'Your Dame Claire isn't ill, is she?' she asked with a warmth that might have been actual concern. But unknown nuns asking hospitality were hardly likely to be of any concern beyond the slightest to her, and Frevisse answered with restraint, 'Only weary with walking, my lady.'

'And that's not surprising. St Frideswide's is no little distance from here. How long have you been on the way? Edeyn may have said, but I've forgotten.'

What else had Mistress Knyvett said? Frevisse gave her and Giles an acknowledging inclination of her head as she answered, 'Three days, but we've not made haste about it, my lady.'

'Nor is there need to, I suppose, when the weather has been so fine.' Lady Lovell's dark eyes were warm with sudden amusement. 'But may I ask if your coming Minster Lovell way has anything to do with this trouble between our stewards over Prior Byfield's well?'

Frevisse's first impulse was to hide her surprise that Lady Lovell knew of it at all, but the merriment in Lady Lovell's face told she knew she had surprised her; and Frevisse, warmed with her infectious amusement, laughed, 'Yes, it would. Is it that notorious a matter?'

'I'd a letter from one of our stewards yesterday. One of his regular reports, not about the well in particular. He'd heard word what Domina – Alys it is now, isn't it? – intended, so when I heard you were from St Frideswide's, I assumed you were the nuns she'd sent.'

'We've a letter and other things for my Lord Lovell from our prioress. We're to speak to him about them and then we'll be on our way.'

'You are welcome to stay as long as necessary, and certainly until you're rested enough to go on in comfort. But I'm afraid my lord husband isn't here and it's with me you'll have to deal.'

'Lord Lovell isn't here?' The last word there had been was that he would be at Minster Lovell until at least midsummer.

'Complications at court.' Lady Lovell gestured with both hands to show how expectations must alter in an instant when there were complications at court. 'Normandy again. He's been summoned to advise my lord of Warwick.'

'Has there been trouble?' Frevisse asked with quick concern.

'Out of the ordinary?' she added, and Lady Lovell's mouth quirked in answering appreciation of the distinction. The war in France was a fitful thing. It was almost ten years since the French witch had nearly overset English power there, and nearly two years since the Burgundians had treacherously deserted to the Dauphin. That had not proved as immediately disastrous as feared, but word could come so slowly to St Frideswide's that there could easily have been some great trouble lately of which they had not yet heard.

But Lady Lovell said, 'No, nothing beyond the ordinary. But the Duke of York has refused to have his governorship extended.'

'He's only held it a year,' Frevisse protested.

'And not been given power or money enough to do much of anything in that while.' Lady Lovell lowered her voice and leaned forward, so that what she said would go no further than Frevisse, Edeyn, and Giles. 'And I gather that being saddled with the Earl of Suffolk ever since last summer is what used up his patience altogether. He's hardly allowed to make a move except that Suffolk approves it and Suffolk approves of very little.'

'Why make York governor and then keep him from doing aught except what Suffolk says he may?' Frevisse asked.

Giles, busy until then with plucking blades of grass and letting them fall, put in, 'Because the royal council – and the king if he has any wit at all – aren't dim enough to trust the Duke of York with that sort of power unchecked.'

'This is the first such office he's been given, and he's young for it, some felt,' Lady Lovell said more moderately.

'What they meant is that he's too royal for it,' Giles returned bitingly. 'If they're that shy of him, they should put him in a cell and forget him rather than give him France and an army.'

'Oh, look at Lionel with Fidelitas!' Edeyn said.

He was holding the ball above the white dog's head; the dog, on its slender hind legs, was dancing upright, trying to reach it.

'Lionel, here!' Edeyn called, and Lionel with a grin tossed her the ball. Fidelitas scrambled after it, then reversed course as Edeyn tossed it back.

'I think you've stolen my dog, Lionel,' Lady Lovell said. 'She's never been that merry with anyone.'

Stroking the dog's smooth, round head while holding the ball for it to chew on, Lionel answered, 'She's a delight. One of Blanche's get?'

'Her last litter.'

Talk went to dogs for a while, and it became clear to Frevisse that Edeyn in particular but Lionel, too, and Giles almost as much, were familiar in the Lovell household. At the same time, Lady Lovell made sure she was not shut out by their familiarity, drawing her to talk of any dogs she might have known. The pleasant while was interrupted by a servant coming from the house to bow to Lady Lovell with apologies and a problem. Lady Lovell asked pardon of her guests with a smile, and Edeyn promptly rose, taking Frevisse and Giles with her. Giles wandered off and Frevisse for wont of certainty what else to do followed Edeyn over to Lionel and the dog.

'She's certainly taken to you,' Edeyn said.

'She has indeed.' Lionel seemed inordinately pleased, as if a friend, even in dog shape, was an unusual pleasure. Edeyn reached to pet the dog, but it shied away from her, not unfriendly but busy pawing at Lionel's arm and whining in a small way at his face, apparently wanting him to toss the ball again. Lionel obligingly tossed it away, but Fidelitas only glanced at it and went on pawing. 'Ah, well,' Lionel said philosophically. 'Time for a new game, it seems.'

'You haven't seen the rose garden, have you?' Edeyn asked Frevisse. 'You must. Lionel, come with us.'

He came, and Fidelitas with him, following as Edeyn led the way into the arbour close at hand. It made the fourth side of the greensward and because it caught the southward sun so fully, was already closely grown, a green-walled, green-roofed world of its own. From the garden side the only way in was through a trellised archway in the middle of it but from there someone could go right or left to reach the two openings on its other side to whatever lay beyond. Edeyn went eagerly, knowing what was there, and brought them out onto another greensward, smaller than the one they had left, enclosed more narrowly by the high manor walls on three sides, by the arbour on the fourth. Small daisies starred its grass and at its centre was a low-rimmed fountain. Around the three walled sides ran a turf-built bench wide enough for sitting and with a trellis made close up against the walls and thickly grown with what Frevisse recognized were rose bushes, more rose bushes than she had ever seen in any one place before. They were yet a month or more from blooming, but when they did, there with the walls to hold in the sunlight and warmth, the garden would be rich with their colour and scent. Her imagination caught at the loveliness of it. The fountain, quiet now, would play in the sunlight, and there would be music and laughter and the light talk of people at ease, at home here.

By then she would be back in St Frideswide's, under Domina Alys's hard eye and harsh tongue. The contrast momentarily irked, but before she could follow the feeling anywhere, Edeyn exclaimed, 'Isn't it wonderful? Lord Lovell has had a tomb made in the church for himself with his effigy and arms and all on it, but Lady Lovell said that instead of an effigy of herself, she'd rather have the money for her garden, and he gave it to her.'

'And she did this?' Frevisse asked, delighted.

Edeyn nodded with answering delight. 'She said she would rather have beauty around her now than a cold stone shape of herself for others to look at after she was gone.'

'A reminder of the beauties of Heaven so she would try harder to reach there, she said,' Lionel added.

'I well believe in the beauties of Heaven,' Frevisse answered, 'but this makes me think of *The Romance of the Rose*, alas for the good of my soul.'

'But isn't the rose supposed to be a symbol of the pure love of Christ?' Lionel returned.

Drily Frevisse answered, 'There are several possible opinions on that.'

Lionel and Edeyn laughed in ready understanding of what she meant. *The Romance of the Rose*, that very long and popular poem, could be taken two widely different ways, with the lover's quest for the rose seen either as his pursuit of Christ's love or else as his lust for a lady's body. It all depended on which way one chose to read the poem.

They had been walking along the gravelled path that bordered the greensward, with Fidelitas leaping up on the turf bench to run at Lionel's elbow height and down again, still trying to paw at him for more attention. Now Lionel gathered the dog into his arms, a full load but manageable. 'You're a trifler,' he said. Fidelitas licked up at his face. 'No, I've washed it lately. I don't need more.'

He had picked up the ball as they came toward the arbour. Now he tossed it ahead of them and let Fidelitas squirm out of his arms to go after it. They had been walking as they talked, Frevisse and Edeyn on either side of Lionel who now took up the rose theme again with a nod at the rose bushes growing all along the trellised wall. 'So despite what holy thoughts we may have here ourselves,' he said, with an acknowledging gesture to include the three of them together, 'concerning roses and *Roses*, worldly loves and Heaven's joys, do you suppose we should warn Lady Lovell that others may be tempted here to more worldly thoughts than we – and she, of course – in our piety are?'

'Or should we simply accept that we can't answer for other people's thoughts?' asked Edeyn with warm laughter. 'And keep our own as pious as best we can?'

Frevisse lightly matched her with a mock sigh and, 'Alas, that might be best. One can so rarely answer for other people in these matters.'

Lionel, the lightness suddenly gone from him, said, 'But we have to answer for what we do to them. And maybe answer on our souls for what we make them do.'

He was looking toward the further arbour archway, and Frevisse, following his gaze, saw Giles standing there as if he had been watching them for a while, listening, knowing he was unnoticed. Looking quickly back and forth between the men as they looked at one another, Frevisse saw understanding and an acknowledgement in them both of something at which she could not guess.

Edeyn, too concentrated on Lionel, saw only his sudden change from happiness and laid a hand on his arm.

'Edeyn,' Giles said, with an amusement as difficult to read as the look that had held between him and Lionel.

Edeyn smiled in greeting, her hand dropping naturally away from Lionel's arm as she asked, 'You've come to call us in to supper?'

'At long last, yes,' Giles answered. 'We're to sit at high table with my lady. You nuns, too,' he added.

Frevisse started, 'Then I'd best go see how Dame Claire does, if she—' but beside her Lionel came to an abrupt stop, staring at his left hand, holding it out in front of him as if it were suddenly not part of him. Fidelitas, the ball dropped and forgotten, whined up at him. Edeyn on his other side, staring first at his face and then at his hand, began, 'Oh, Lionel—'

He stopped her with a curt shake of his head, his attention still on his hand as he ordered, 'You go on. There's time yet. I'll go to our room. There's nothing else can be done. Go on.'

'I'll send Martyn to you.'

'If he isn't there, yes.' He was curt, not looking at her or anyone, only at his hand as if he hated it. Or feared it.

Giles came to take Edeyn's arm. 'He's told you what he wants.

Come on then.' Whatever Giles felt, it was not pain or anything like sympathy. 'My lady,' he added to Frevisse, 'if you would?' Indicating she should come with them.

Frevisse hesitated, but Lionel wanted to be left and she went, wondering what was toward, wondering why Edeyn, like Lionel, had gone pale and now was silent, her husband's hand still around her arm as if to be sure she went with him as they crossed the gardens back toward the manor house, Lionel left behind to come alone.

Chapter 5

GILES STOOD WITH his back pressed against their room's door, as far from the thing on the floor as he could be and still be in the room at all. Good old Lionel had made it to their room before the attack came on him. How pleasant for him, and for everyone else who was therefore spared the sight of it. Giles had managed for almost three years now to avoid seeing Lionel in one of his fits and he would have gladly made it longer, but this one might give him the chance he wanted. Somewhere other than Minster Lovell might have been better, but if the chance was going to be now, he would take it. He was tired of waiting. But to know if this was the one he could use, he had to be here and see it.

He had waited until he was sure Lionel would be down and unknowing before he came, and then said he was there because Edeyn had been worried. Martyn could not order him away and he had stayed, just as he meant to. The room was a goodly one, agreeable and, Giles had noticed at the very first, well apart from most of the household, near only Lady Lovell's parlour and the chapel. Chosen, he suspected, so that as few folk as necessary would know if one of Lionel's fits came on him. Its only lack was bar or lock for the door to keep someone coming in unwanted, and here was Lionel in full grunt and thrash on the floor, with Martyn trying to keep him from hitting himself against the bed foot or too hard on the floor, unable to watch the door, too, so that it was not unreasonable for Giles to have stayed once he was in, to guard the door as a 'kindness' to his cousin, he would have explained if he had been asked, but Martyn had not bothered, the arrogant bastard.

Holding down his gorge, Giles glanced at Lionel and away again. There was nothing human left there on the floor, just a writhing, twisting, grunting hulk, all drool and twitching. If ever Lionel had clear knowledge of what he was when a fit came on him, he would have shut himself up to die and been done with it. But he did not know and he never would if Martyn had his way. Dog-vomit Martyn would keep him ignorant of it to doomsday and protect him as much as might be in the bargain because Martyn would be out of his profitable place if anything permanent happened to Lionel, damn them both.

Between them, Martyn and Edeyn were forever protecting Lionel from seeing what he was – a long-jawed, scar-faced, shambling farce of a man living out a sham of a life to everyone's inconvenience. Why Martyn did it was plain enough. Lionel was profit to him and a sure place in life. It was Edeyn who was hard to understand. To Edeyn Lionel was ... what? Giles had never quite been certain, but it was sure she had never seen him in writhe and spasm on a floor, never seen him as he fully was. She only knew he was 'afflicted', and so in need of her woman-hearted sympathy. But then, she was so soft she had even spent hours nursing her sick greyhound bitch last winter when any a fool could tell it was going to die. When he had had enough, he had put the bitch out of its misery and everybody's way with a heavy pillow. It had been a mercy all around, for everyone, but Edeyn had taken it like a woman, badly and with tears, and then, like a woman, in a few days forgotten all about it. She had even forgotten to ask him for the dog he had promised her in the bitch's place.

It would go the same with her over Lionel. Grief and misery for a while and then she would forget. The baby would be a distraction, too. She'd not be thinking of much else in a while.

That was one of the useful things about women: give them sport in bed and set them breeding and they were satisfied until it was time to do it to them again.

He chanced another glance at Lionel. The fit was nearly done. The thrash and writhe were fallen away to only twitching. Soon he would lie quiet and then rouse, a little more witless than usual and exhausted for a while but no great harm done. By the time the rest of them came in at evening's end, Martyn would have seen him clean and into bed to sleep it off. But there would be tomorrow. Tomorrow night probably, if the pattern held. The fit had been a brief one and that meant that almost assuredly tomorrow night – pray God not sooner – Lionel would have one of the great ones, the wildly violent ones that left him nigh to mindless with exhaustion for hours afterwards.

Exactly as Giles needed him to be.

Chapter 6

WHEN SUPPER WAS finished in the great hall, household and guests rose from the benches and moved aside for the hall servants first to clear away the food and dishes and tablecloths and then the tables themselves, opening the hall for whatever the household chose to do with the evening – talk or singing or dancing.

Left to her own choice, Frevisse would have been satisfied to seek out the manor chapel, said Compline with Dame Claire, and been gladly done with the day. But it was not her choice. Lady Lovell had been gracious enough to do her and Dame Claire the honour of having them sit at the high table. They must be gracious in return, which meant joining in at least the evening's conversation. Not the singing nor the dancing assuredly, but at least the talk.

In the general shift of folk while the servants cleared the hall of all but the chairs and benches left for comfort, she drifted apart from Dame Claire who had fallen into talk over supper with one of Lady Lovell's older ladies about the particular benefits of certain herbs. There presently seemed to be a cheerful disagreement over whether camomile or dandelion was the better at cleansing the body of certain phlegms, and because she had no idea on the matter either way, Frevisse did not care to join in. Dame Claire was better for her sleep, her colour good again and the stiffness that had had her limping when she first arose gone by the time they had come down to the hall. It had occurred to Frevisse, finding she could not remember when last Dame Claire had been out of St Frideswide's further than Prior Byfield, to be worried for her, surrounded in the hall by far more people and overt cheerfulness than she was used to. There had been people, strangers, through these few days of travel but only a few at any time, not a great clutter and noise of them like here, eager for the evening's pleasures at an hour when in St Frideswide's the nuns were turning toward the quietness of Compline's prayers and bed.

But Dame Claire seemed to be enjoying herself and so did the lady with her, so Frevisse left them to it and looked down the hall in search of John Naylor. He had been seated at a lower table in company and deep conversation with an older man whom Frevisse guessed by his quiet manner of authority and his being sat with John to be Lord Lovell's high steward. It had crossed her mind to hope that young John was aware that what he might say could affect their later dealings on the nunnery's matter, but while she watched he had seemed to be listening far more than he was talking and she had been reassured. He was more likely to make a good impression that way than another.

But she still wanted to learn what had been said and was making her way among the people toward where she had last seen him when Master Geffers, the franklin, intercepted her. Without his regrettable hat his presence was diminished and his years more obvious, but his inclination to talk was the same as he slid from between two men into Frevisse's way with, 'Dame Frevisse, we meet again.'

Frevisse acknowledged that truth with a brief inclination of her head and attempted to go on past him, but he was too much in the way and already chatting with great enthusiasm about how splendid Minster Lovell was and, 'I understand you and Dame Claire are staying with Lady Lovell's damsels. How very good of Lady Lovell, very good.'

From wariness of anything that might prolong the conversation, Frevisse did not ask where he had been given quarters, but that did not stop him from telling her he was above and beyond the kitchens. 'And very pleasant it is. Though not so good as what there will be when the west range is finished. There'll be a great many pleasant rooms there, I understand.'

Frevisse thought that Master Geffers probably *understood* very little. He was just skilled at collecting oddments of information and pasting them together into what passed for conversation. She knew his sort and how little chance she had of escaping him without some sort of talk, so she asked, 'And the Stenbys. Where are they?' She had not thought of them between when they had parted company on the road and now, but they served to divert Master Geffers.

'Ah, the Stenbys. There's a pair I'd not mind on my properties. Solid yeomen. No nonsense and good workers, if I'm any judge. They're not here. They found a place to stay in the village. Some goodwife glad of an extra halfpenny for putting them up and feeding them. They'll make their devotion at the shrine in the morning and start home afterwards.' Master Geffers leaned closer to Frevisse's ear as if someone in the shift of folk around them might be interested in the great secret he was about to impart. 'A wise choice for them. They'd not have fitted in here. Best among their own kind.'

Frevisse made – murmured was too kind a word; muttered was closer to the truth – some sort of agreement at him and moved on among the people talking and waiting around them for the last of the trestles to be carried out. She was no longer particularly set on finding John so much as on escaping Master Geffers; but Master Geffers, probably out of long experience of people trying to escape him, kept with her, saying as they went, 'And you'll have noticed that Master Knyvet isn't here, either.'

The eagerness behind his words warned Frevisse there was a particularly choice piece of talk to come, and she cast quickly through her mind for a way to avoid it. She liked what little she had seen of Lionel Knyvet. She did not want to hear about him by way of Master Geffers's tattling, but Master Geffers's tongue was too quick for her. He shook his head and said with a regret that Frevisse doubted went further than the turned-down corners of his mouth, 'There's a sad case. Poor man. We were warned but one always hopes, but I fear the worst, not seeing him here for supper.'

Before she could help herself, Frevisse asked, 'Warned?'

'About his affliction.' Master Geffers dropped his voice unnecessarily low, as if everyone around them was waiting eagerly to hear what he said. 'He's possessed, you know. Horribly. Since childhood.'

Frevisse crossed herself even as she protested, 'Possessed? How?'

'By a demon.'

Of course by a demon, Frevisse wanted to snap at him. What else would he be possessed by? But Master Geffers was going on, gathering speed now that he had her attention. 'It's why he's making this pilgrimage around to St Kenelm's shrines. Over the past years he's gone everywhere, prayed everywhere, made gifts to saints from one end of England to the other, but no one and nothing has been able to free him.' Master Geffers nodded, solemn faced with the weight of it, but it was avid delight that gleamed in his eyes. 'Fits. He has fits. The falling sickness, you know. The demon seizes him and he loses all control. He flails, thrashes, spits, blasphemes God's name and everything holy. He—'

'You've seen this?'

Master Geffers hastily crossed himself. 'God forbid, no. But I was told by someone who's seen it a hundred times and done what he could to help.'

'Who?' Frevisse snapped, angry on Lionel Knyvet's behalf that whatever happened to him was reduced to greedy talk in Master

Geffers's busy mouth by someone who should have known better.

Her tone was lost on Master Geffers. Urged on by her interest, he said, 'His own cousin. Master Giles Knyvet. Who would know better? He's seen the demon take him with his own eyes.'

'And he told you about it? Does Master Knyvet want this thing known all over? Surely he doesn't.'

Master Geffers agreed to that readily. 'Oh, of course he doesn't. He keeps it secret as best he may. But we were travelling together, you see. What if an attack came and we had no warning? Master Giles wanted us prepared. For our own safety. The attacks are so violent and come so suddenly. Though mind you' – he leaned toward her, drawn by his avidity to tell – 'he does have warning, Master Giles says. The demon taunts him, to add to the torment. It tickles in his left hand before it attacks. So if ever you see Master Knyvet look at his left hand oddly, leave him as quickly as you may.'

Frevisse remembered Lionel's face in the garden as he had held out his hand to look at it as if it were no longer part of him. He must have been feeling the demon then. Carefully she asked, 'Where is he now?'

'That's the question, isn't it? He takes the warning and finds some place alone before the fit comes on him, with only his man Martyn Gravesend to see him through it. A pushing fellow, that Martyn, taking every advantage of his master's curse to put himself forward. And as damned as the demon itself or he'd never dare to face the fits out the way he does. That's what Master Giles says.'

Master Giles would say that, Frevisse thought. He had been quick enough to make his escape, she realized, to leave his cousin alone when he knew what was coming on him.

But Lionel had wanted them to go. He had wanted to be left, to not be seen. The warning in his hand gave him time for that and in that much it was a blessing.

But that was not the way Giles had made it seem when he had seen fit to tell Master Geffers and apparently the Stenbys. Or else that was not the way Master Geffers had heard it.

Revolted both by the idea of Lionel seized in a demon-fit and by Master Geffers's eager talk of it, Frevisse asked, 'Giles told all of you that were travelling together? The Stenbys, too?'

'All of us, to be sure. And said I should warn my servant, too, just in case.'

A servant who probably talked as readily as Master Geffers did, so that in a day or so there would be no one here who would not be watching for Lionel to look at his left hand oddly, with the worst of them hoping he would. And although Master Geffers would go on his way tomorrow morning, he would surely go on talking about Lionel along his way. Having travelled with someone possessed by a demon was too prime a tale to go untold. Frevisse wondered if Giles fully knew how much a cruelty he had done Lionel with his 'warning'.

Remembering even what little she had so far seen of Giles, she rather thought he did.

A servant in the Lovell livery bowed in front of her and said, 'My lady asks if you'd join her for the evening, my lady.'

Frevisse was glad to accept, both because it offered Lady Lovell's pleasant company and an escape from Master Geffers. With a murmured farewell to the franklin, she followed the servant away among the cheerful crowding of household folk, asking as they went, 'Were you to find my companion, Dame Claire, too?'

'She and Lady Elizabeth have already gone, my lady,' the man answered.

Frevisse noticed that most of the folk still here had been at the lower tables. Lady Lovell, her ladies, and what gentlemen there had been were gone, apparently as usual. The man led her deftly among the others, back to the dais and to the door at its opposite end from where Luce had taken them that afternoon. Beyond it

was a small antechamber with doors on each side of it, the one to
the left shut, the one at its far end open to a spiral stairway almost
lost in the unlighted shadows, the one on their right open to
lamplight. The man rapped lightly on the frame of the open door
and stood aside, looking back, for her to go past him.

The room she entered was large, low-ceilinged, pleasantly
proportioned, with its three wide, stone-mullioned windows
looking out on the garden where a clear blue twilight still
lingered. Lamps set about on shoulder-tall, wrought-iron holders
showed golden rush-matting covering the floor and the ceiling
beams brightly painted in a weave of vines and flowers. Gaily
embroidered cushions were strewn along the wide bench below
the windows, and girls and women vaguely familiar from that
afternoon in the garden and a few gentlemen Frevisse remembered from the hall at supper sat there and on other, larger
cushions around the floor in talk and laughter. Opposite the
windows a fireplace with elaborately carven stone mantel
emboldened the wall. Lady Lovell sat in front of it on a long,
backed, cushioned wooden bench, with Edeyn seated beside her,
and Giles, Father Henry, the house priest, and Dame Claire
standing near.

From the doorway, Frevisse's guide made a low bow and said,
'My lady.'

Lady Lovell smiled and held out a hand in welcome. 'Good, he
found you! Come join us, please. We lost you in the hall.'

Drawn easily into her company, Frevisse noted first that Dame
Claire was apparently at ease and then that Father Henry and
Sire Benedict were enjoying talk of their own to one side of
everyone else's. Something about St Augustine, she thought from
a snatch she overheard. She had not thought Father Henry would
remember so much of his studies as even to recall St Augustine,
let alone discuss him.

That was a mean-spirited thought, she realized in the same
moment as she had it; but before she could follow where it had

come from, John Naylor came in with the man he had been with at supper. They bowed to Lady Lovell without approaching and moved away into one of the groups across the room. Frevisse noted where, with intent to talk with young John before the evening was done. For now it was enough that for the first time since coming to Minster Lovell, she knew where all of their company was and how they seemed to be.

In something like an echo to her thought, she heard Lady Lovell saying, 'We're a sadly diminished company, I fear, with my lord and so many of the men gone with him, and no notion of how long they'll be about it.'

'Is it going to be complicated?' Edeyn asked.

'If it involves France and money, it's always complicated,' her husband pointed out, and there was wry, agreeing laughter among them.

'Dame Frevisse told me a little of what's toward,' Dame Claire said. 'Is there trouble?'

'Mostly only for my lord of Warwick.' Lady Lovell shook her head. 'He really does not want the office or to go to France. There's rumour that he's ill, would prefer to take to his bed. But King Henry is insisting on it. So he's called various of his people to him for advice on what to expect and what to ask of the king before he agrees, as agree he must. Hence, my lord is gone.'

'Your husband served in France,' Dame Claire said. 'For a long while, I think?'

'Long enough to know he doesn't desire to go back. But then there's this that came from it.' Lady Lovell looked around at her rich room, with the sense of all of Minster Lovell that lay beyond it. 'His profits from France have helped to build all this without too deeply draining regular revenues from our lands, so we've little cause of complaint, I suppose. So long as he doesn't have to go back,' she added with a laugh.

The talk moved along easy ways to nowhere in particular. Weather and crops and pilgrimages and how the roads were.

Father Henry and Sire Benedict wandered away with whatever they were discussing, and eventually Frevisse was sitting at one end of the long bench beside Edeyn who turned away from Dame Claire and Lady Lovell's deep conversation over which herbs companioned well with others in a garden to ask, 'You're well recovered from your walking?'

'Very well, thank you. I have to confess we've not been striving to see how many miles we can make but rather taking our time.'

'But it isn't going so well for Dame Claire, is it?' Edeyn asked with concern. 'She's not so used to it?'

The girl's perception surprised Frevisse. She had been seeing Edeyn as more a girl than a woman because she seemed uncalloused yet by the pains life would bring, still holding to that wonderful belief of the young that they could not be touched by the worst things in life. Not a belief that lasted but potentially immensely aggravating while it did. Probably much of her innocence came from the simple fact that she had had no children yet; and she was likely protected by her husband and even Lionel from full understanding of what Lionel's affliction meant, even though she and her husband lived with him.

But to Edeyn's question about Dame Claire, Frevisse said mildly, 'No, she's not. Nor am I of late, come to that, but I had more of such walking in my girlhood and the way of it comes back to me when needed.'

Edeyn asked more questions then, careful ones that showed she was ready to pull back if she were shown she went too far, but Frevisse talked a little to her about a childhood spent on roads across England and through Europe, until Edeyn sighed and said, 'I've never really been anywhere. There was home and then here, around to their manors with my lord and lady, and once to London, and now we go between Knyvet and Langling every year, but that's all.'

'And hither, thither, and yon on Lionel's pilgrimages these three years we've been married, don't forget,' her husband put in from where he leaned on his crossed arms on the high back of the bench behind her. 'Not that those are any great delight. Monks and shrines and too much praying.' He bowed slightly to Frevisse and added with a smile, 'Begging your pardon of course.'

Frevisse, in mind of what she had heard from Master Geffers about him, found neither his smile nor him charming. She replied, 'A pity, though, that his pilgrimages have done him so little good. Master Geffers was talking in the hall about what happens to him. That was an attack coming on him in the garden, wasn't it?'

She had been wrong about Edeyn. The girl's stricken expression and her involuntary, almost angry half turn toward her husband betrayed she was far from untouched by what happened to Lionel.

But it was Giles whom Frevisse was set at now and she pushed on with, 'How does he?' and saw that her directness made no noticeable impression on Giles. He only shrugged and answered, 'Well enough. The fit was a brief one. He's sleeping it off now, with his knave Martyn hovering over him. That man was born to be a nursemaid. And a scavenging hound. He's found his garbage heap in Lionel, that's for certain.'

That sounded like a song often sung and one Giles would have gone on with, but Edeyn interrupted him, asking Frevisse, 'Master Geffers told you about Lionel?'

'When I talked with him in the hall after supper. He seemed to know all about it.'

Edeyn looked up at Giles. 'You told him, didn't you?' Giles shrugged, dismissing what was close to an angry accusation, but Edeyn said, the accusation more open, 'That was unkind. The man talks. Everyone will know.'

'Everyone here knows anyway. Why do you think we have the room we do?'

'Because until the west range is done, I have none better to offer a loved guest like Edeyn,' Lady Lovell said, turning from her conversation with Dame Claire.

Giles and Edeyn had kept their voices down to polite quietness. Skill both in keeping conversations private and in not heeding others' talk was needed with so many living together, but they were too near Lady Lovell's shoulder to have been unheard, and because she was their lady, she did not need to ignore them unless she wished. She smiled at them both and said, 'You're worried over Lionel?'

'He's been attacked again, my lady,' Edeyn said softly. 'It had been two months or more. We'd hoped—'

'You'd hoped,' Giles interrupted. 'The rest of us know better.'

Lady Lovell fixed her eyes on him in a look more sharp than Frevisse would have cared to have used on her, but her tone was mild enough as she said, 'We pray and we hope, Master Giles. That's how things change in this world.'

Giles immediately bowed his head to her in gracious acceptance. 'You have the right of it, my lady. I've been too close to it too long. Hope grows thin after so many disappointments. That's all.'

'Master Knyvet is afflicted?' Dame Claire asked. 'With what?'

'The falling sickness,' Lady Lovell said.

'Ah, poor man. For how long? What's been done for him?'

'Everything that's ever been known,' Lady Lovell said.

'Concoctions, decoctions, electuaries, pilgrimages, prayers,' Giles put in. 'A fortune's been spent on it, first by his father and now by him.'

'And none of it to any use?' Dame Claire asked.

'As you see, he's not with us tonight.'

'Has pennyroyal been tried? Saffron, I've heard, can help. It's expensive but very little is needed.' Almost to herself, her mind away on possibilities, she added, 'But then only a very little is safe to use, I understand.'

'If we could make his demon down a medicine direct, it might effect a difference,' Giles said drily. 'On Lionel there's been none.'

Drifting while they talked, the house priest Sire Benedict and Father Henry had come back to them in time for just that last. 'Demon?' Father Henry asked, hearing enough to catch his interest. 'No difference? What?'

'My cousin,' Giles said. 'He's—'

'Giles!' Edeyn protested.

He gave her a look affectionate and lightly mocking. 'You think he's never going to hear?'

Lady Lovell took her hand with a sympathy that made no effort to stop Giles because he was right. The only surprise was that Sire Benedict had not talked of it already. Everyone else did at the first chance they had, Frevisse thought angrily, then chided herself because that was not fair, only her own ill temper at Giles coming to the fore. He was enjoying himself and not even particularly trying to hide it.

'My cousin has the falling sickness. Every so often a demon-fit comes on him. He's in one right now. That's why he wasn't at supper.'

'It's over with!' Edeyn said. 'He's only worn out now, with fighting it so hard.'

Her protest skimmed past Father Henry unheeded as he asked while crossing himself, 'That's why he's on pilgrimage then, is it? Though I'd think he'd seek out St Vitus instead of Kenelm.' He turned to Sire Benedict. 'Wouldn't you? For the falling sickness? But I don't know of any shrine off-hand.'

'I've heard of one at Corvey, I think,' Sire Benedict said.

'You mean Corby, in Lincolnshire?' Father Henry said doubtfully.

'No, Corvey. It's abroad. Somewhere beyond France?' Sire Benedict was unsure, too. Farther than anyone was likely to go at any rate.

'But exorcism. That's been done, hasn't it?' Father Henry asked.

'Several times,' Giles answered. 'It works as well as everything else does.'

'But which phase of the moon?' Father Henry asked. 'Not the new? I've heard tell of a house exorcized when the moon was new and it burned down the week after, with everyone in it.'

'The body being house of the soul this while that it lives, it would be the same case,' Sire Benedict agreed. 'It wasn't done at the new moon, was it?'

'I don't remember,' Giles said with more seeming seriousness than before. 'Though now that I think on it, it was after the last exorcism that he fell headforemost nearly into the fire. That scar on his face, you know. That's from that.'

The priests shook their heads, Sire Benedict clicking his tongue.

Giles was not the only one enjoying himself, Frevisse thought bitterly. From Master Geffers's plain-faced tale-bearing to all these various considerations of herbs and prayers and exorcisms, everyone had their own way of taking pleasure for themselves, one way or another, out of Lionel's curse. Except for Edeyn and maybe Lady Lovell, no one seemed to see him as the charming man who had welcomed strangers to his company along the wayside this afternoon, who laughed over silly riddles and walked in a rose garden talking of a poem. No one seemed to remember any of that about him, only that he was demon-ridden. The thing that was least himself was the only thing about him people thought of.

Except for Edeyn and probably Lady Lovell, which spoke well of both of them. Except that for Edeyn, Lionel was very near. Their laughter and their pleasures matched each other and what might that not lead to, if it had not already?

Frevisse realized abruptly that she was going the way of malicious conjecture herself, and it did not matter that it was only in her own thoughts rather than with her tongue, it was something in which she should not indulge, any more than the eager talk around her – gone now to discussion between Dame Claire and Sire Benedict of what herbs might work best in conjunction with the efforts of exorcism – should lead her to indulge in anger at anyone. Including Giles.

'Excuse me,' she said, rose and made curtsy to Lady Lovell, and crossed the room to where young John Naylor and the other man still stood in talk.

They dropped whatever they were talking about to step apart and each bow to her. She inclined her head to them in return and then more particularly to the older man as young John introduced them, 'Dame Frevisse, Master Holt, Lord Lovell's high steward.'

So she had been right about that. This was the man who oversaw all the men who oversaw all the numerous Lovell properties. He was perhaps near fifty, with grey and dark mixed thoroughly together in his hair and the years lined strongly, pleasantly in his face, as if he were someone who did well a job he cared about.

She smiled at both of them and said, 'I haven't had chance to ask how it goes with you, John. You're well seen to?'

'Very well,' he said eagerly. 'Master Holt has seen to me himself.'

'Thank you for that courtesy,' Frevisse said.

'I know his uncle a little. It's pleasure as well as courtesy,' Master Holt said. He cocked an eye toward the seat she had just left. 'I think the talk there didn't suit you?'

She did not want to begin again on Lionel and so made do with a part truth. 'I'm afraid Giles Knyvet grates on me. I found I was wanting to be rude to him and decided a change of conversation might save my manners. At least I could be rude *about* him instead of to his face.'

Both men smiled appreciatively. 'You're not alone in not much liking him,' Master Holt said.

He might have let it go at that, but young John put in, 'Petir in the stable, when we first came in and I was seeing to the horses, was a-cursing that Master Giles was come. He'd been in service in the Knyvet stables, and Master Giles claimed he was annoying Mistress Edeyn by too close attentions and had him dismissed when it wasn't true.'

'Or so Petir says,' Master Holt said. 'Right now Petir is taking daily posies to one of the dairy maids. He's soft where women are concerned. He may well have been too inclined to Mistress Edeyn and shown it more than Master Giles cared for.'

'But Petir says it wasn't really for that but because he saw Giles cutting a holly stick and told Master Gravesend of it because he knew what Master Giles meant to do with it.'

'And what did he mean to do with it?' Frevisse asked. 'According to Petir.'

'According to Petir, he's quick to strike servants who displease him, and he looks for reasons to be displeased. Usually only his own servants, but not always. And if anyone complains, he sees to it something more happens to them. He usually uses no more than a switch, but Petir saw him cutting the holly and told Master Gravesend.'

Frevisse and Master Holt exchanged glances. It was one thing to lay a birch switch across a servant, or even, if the case warranted it, a cane; but a holly stick was something else altogether. There was no give to a holly stick. It struck and it bruised, and the bruise went so deep that it was unlawful to strike pigs with it because the hurt flesh would not take salt and cure for winter storage but rot instead. The hurt would be the same on human flesh, deep and lasting.

'So he told Master Gravesend and then there was trouble and at the end of it Petir was let go,' Master Holt guessed.

'That's what Petir says. He also says he was glad to go because he didn't want to be there to find out what Master Giles might do against him in return.'

To Frevisse's mind that suited well with what she so far knew of Giles. Cruelties against his cousin behind his back, more overt cruelties against those who had small defence against him.

And here she was caught up in talk again about people who were no concern of hers, she reminded herself, and was relieved that Dame Claire joined them then. She was introduced to Master Holt and exchanged greetings but said with a smile, 'I was wondering if we should go to the chapel for Compline now, Dame Frevisse?'

They should. It was a good thought and a welcome way out and Frevisse agreed to it readily. They could even stay there in prayer until they heard the household going to bed and so escape more talk, she thought, as she made farewell to Master Holt and young John and followed Dame Claire away.

'Lady Lovell told me the way,' Dame Claire explained as they left the parlour. 'It's up these stairs here,' – the stairs Frevisse had noticed earlier, going up at the far end of the antechamber. As they went, Dame Claire added, whispering, nodding toward the door opposite the parlour, 'That's Lionel Knyvet's room there.'

Frevisse nodded in reply and held her tongue.

The soft talk and music from the parlour muted as they circled up the dark curve of the stairs. At their top they opened into another small chamber, as unlit as the one below except that the wide door into the chapel itself stood open and, by the faint glow of the altar lamp, they knew which way to turn.

'That way,' Dame Claire said, pointing toward this chamber's far end where the outline of a door barely showed, 'leads back into the solar and the ladies' chamber beyond, so we don't have to go back downstairs and up again.'

That was helpful, at any rate, but Frevisse truly wanted to forget everything and turn her mind to the evening prayers now. She led the way into the chapel and by the altar lamp's small light had an impression of a high beamed ceiling, walls painted with pictures she did not try to make out in the low light, three tall windows of coloured glass and stone fretwork with night's full darkness beyond them. A faintness of music and indistinguishable talk came from below but too remote to be a trouble. The peace of a place meant for prayers wrapped around her, and Dame Claire drew a breath of relief as deep as Frevisse felt. Together they went forward and knelt at the foot of the two steps below the altar on a carpet woven in jewel-rich reds and blues and gold, crossed themselves, and bowed their heads to the welcome familiarity of Compline's prayers.

Chapter 7

THE NIGHT SPENT in the ladies' chamber was not particularly different from one in the nunnery's dormitory, once the bedtime chatter had quieted, and except she was not used to sharing a bed, Frevisse slept well and awoke feeling ready for the day when in the soft light of earliest dawn the ladies began to stir and rise.

She and Dame Claire finished dressing easily before the others, their gowns and headwear meant to be put on without help and quickly. Then they waited, sitting quietly on their bed while the others finished, until Lady Lovell came from her own chamber and they all followed after her through the solar to the chapel for morning mass. Others of the household were there, the chapel fairly full before Sire Benedict, with Father Henry to assist him, began. Frevisse glimpsed Lionel, with Giles and Edeyn, standing to the right of the door and well to the back in the one quick glance she took around. Then she bent her head and mind to prayer, glad to go into the blessed joy where the passing matters of everyday – the concerns that came and briefly were and went away – were put aside and mind and heart given over to worship, to awareness of God's love and the eternity that lay beyond life.

Sire Benedict went through the service without haste or flourish, his firm and careful voice weighted to the solemn wonder of what he dealt with. When he had finished and the flurry of amens and hands moving to cross breasts had shifted to a general movement out of the chapel and down to the great hall for breakfast, Dame Claire and Frevisse stood aside, no need for any word between them, until everyone had gone, including the two priests. Then, the chapel now to themselves, they went forward and knelt before the altar, as they had last night, to say the office of Prime together.

The prayers were a joyful welcome to the day, thanks and hope for it combined; and when at their end, refreshed, Frevisse rose to find her knees stiff from the long kneeling, she was, as almost always, surprised at it, as if somehow her body should have been as far removed from itself as her mind had been. But it never was. It tediously clung to its necessities, day in, day out, and insisted that she heed them, too. She had long since learned to make the adjustment from the delight of reaching out toward God's love, forgetful of the world, to bothering over her body's demands and boring needs, but she would still rather have not been bothered.

Just now, she found, her stomach in particular wanted to be heeded. Possibly in the same straits, Dame Claire, smiling, made the sign for breakfast. The habit of silence was strong in both of them, and Frevisse nodded for answer, smiling back.

They were in time to take bread and ale from the single table set up in the great hall before it was cleared. No benches had been set; no one troubled to sit down over so short a meal. Frevisse and Dame Claire ate standing to one side while the table was taken away and the last lingering folk left. The sun was not yet far enough around to reach the hall's windows but the light of a bright dawn filled it, and from the sounds in the yard outside there was going to be a riding out to somewhere.

Curious and with nothing else they should be doing, Frevisse and Dame Claire went that way, finishing their breakfast as they went and giving their drinking bowls to a servant they met in the screens passage on their way to the outer door. Coming out onto the doorstep, they found perhaps a score of horsemen milling in the centre of the yard, mounted and ready to leave. Their clothing and the horses' harnesses were serviceable rather than rich, showing they were bound for hunting, not a casual ride. Frevisse saw John Naylor was with them, and Giles Knyvet, but if Lionel was, she missed him.

The dawn's light clouds, carried eastward on a gentle breeze, their underbellies gold from the rising sun, were clearing to a pale sky. The morning air was bright and cool, fresh from a small rain in the night. Lady Lovell was standing among her ladies at the yard's edge on the cobbled walk just beyond the door, watching the riders but apparently aware of all else around her because, as Dame Claire and Frevisse came out, she turned to raise her hand to them in welcome. She wore a gown of young green today, the colour suited to the spring morning and her rich, dark eyes and pale skin. She looked as if she meant to go riding, too, her veil and wimple more practical and covering than yesterday's had been, but the horsemen were gathering now behind the huntsman, whatever they had been waiting for finally accomplished, and in a clatter of hoofs and eagerness they all rode out through the cobbled gateway, gone in moments, leaving the yard silent and seeming larger.

'There!' said Lady Lovell. 'That's seen to.' She smiled at Dame Claire and Frevisse. 'They're away to hunt roebuck now it's come into season again and we'd best wish them luck. The larder is low.' She nodded toward the unfinished west range of buildings where the workmen were already moving among the beginnings of walls and piles of stone. 'Feeding them alone is challenge enough, let be the rest of the household.'

She was cheerful over it; and judging by what Frevisse had seen so far of Minster Lovell and its lady, whatever was needful was probably handled well and in good time. But Dame Claire, having been cellarer at St Frideswide's, in charge of its stores and kitchen and aware of the complications of providing for a great many people for a long while, asked, 'What did you do through Lent? Do you have to buy the while or are you able to have stores enough?'

'Two hundred barrels of salt fish in as many different sorts as can be had, bought and brought by Martinmas,' Lady Lovell said. 'And hope we've laid in spices and have herbs enough to change their taste from one day to the next from Shrovetide on,' when hunting and the eating of flesh had to stop until Easter day. 'And bread to balance them. Thank God the harvests have been good of late.'

Dame Claire could give amen to that readily enough. It was only two years since the end of three years of bad harvests when what had grown had rotted. St Frideswide's own fields had not produced enough for the nunnery's needs, and high costs had made buying what little was imported almost ruinous. The same would have been true for every household, even those rich as the Lovells, because money could not buy what was not here.

But that was past. People were well-fleshed again and this year looked to be another goodly one.

Lady Lovell was saying, 'I hope you'll pardon me if I put off our talking over our village matter until afternoon. I'm to ride out this morning to see how it is with the fallow ploughing and commend my dairywomen on how well they're doing. Cook is complaining over what he's to do with all the milk. Make more custards, I tell him. So if you grow sick of having custards while you're here, it's the dairymaids' fault.'

More horses were being brought from the stable, lighter boned than those on which the hunters had ridden out: palfreys for an easy ride around the manor and its fields rather than hard galloping in the woods and over rough ground; and instead of plain harness, their leathers were bright with greens and reds and strong blues, some hung with little bells. Four of Lady Lovell's ladies, Master Holt, and two squires strolled across the yard toward them. Lady Lovell stayed where she was and her horse was brought to her while Dame Claire said for both herself and Frevisse that they were quite willing to wait until her ladyship's convenience in the village matter.

'But this afternoon for certain,' Lady Lovell said. She mounted and added cheerfully, 'Luce, I leave our guests to your care.'

Luce, Dame Claire, and Frevisse curtsied their acknowledgement but she had already drawn her horse around. Bells chimed on its harness as it stepped away, light-footed, leading the small, brightly dressed and caparisoned group away through the gateway.

The women left behind drifted back into the house, Dame Claire and Frevisse following Luce. The others were talking of the duties they were to see to while their lady was gone – Frevisse gathered that Lady Lovell left them to no idleness – and though some scattered away through the house about their business, Luce followed three others back into the hall and across it to Lady Lovell's parlour, with Frevisse and Dame Claire perforce with her. They were no more bent on idleness than the rest. In the parlour they all took sewing from a chest along one wall, and while the others moved away to sit where the light was best, beside the windows, Luce asked Frevisse and Dame Claire, 'Would you care to join us? We're sewing things for my dower chest. My lady said we could work at them this morning, please you.'

Sewing and Frevisse had never done well together, but Dame Claire said readily they would be most happy to join in so there was no help for it. She made the best of it by offering to do hems and was set to turning under and stitching the hem of a white linen smock while Dame Claire gladly took to setting in a gown's sleeve and Luce worked on a bodice.

Dame Claire commented on the good quality of the cloth. Luce explained it was a gift from Lady Lovell. 'She's very good to any of us when we come to marriage.'

'Remember how after everything else she'd done, she gave

Constance a set of strings for her lute when Constance was crying, so sure there would be none to be had where she going to live in the Welsh Marches?' one of the other women said.

'And then it all turned out badly, with her husband dying before two years were out and no babies either,' someone else said.

'No ill luck on me,' Luce said quickly, signing a cross in the air between her and the other woman.

Several of them paused to cross and uncross their fingers before one of them said, 'But I don't know that Constance thought it ill luck, come to that. Your fellow is young enough but Constance's husband was well toward the grave and two wives there before him when the match was made.'

'The Lovells are very good at helping their people to marriages if our families ask,' Luce explained. 'They've property in so many places and know so many folk, there's almost always a match they can at least suggest if not arrange.'

'There's one they did well for.' A woman further along the window seat nodded out into the garden. Frevisse looked up from her laborious hemming to see Edeyn strolling along one of the formal garden paths, Lionel beside her, Martyn and the white dog following.

'Except for him of course,' another of the women said, with a meaningful nod at Lionel.

'But it's not as if she were married to him,' Luce said warmly. 'No one tried to do that to her.'

'Nobody would!' the other woman exclaimed. 'And they couldn't anyway. He's vowed never to marry, they say. So his cousin will inherit eventually, and that means she's as good as lady of the Knyvet lands already.'

'With a husband I'd not mind being in bed with,' the further lady said.

'I'd guess she doesn't either. At any rate, she's with child.'

Exclaims of delight greeted that.

'But can you imagine having a baby in a house with someone like that?' Luce asked. Her voice thrilled with a horror made pleasurable because it was something she did not have to face.

'Can you imagine even walking with him the way she is?' the other woman said. 'She's braver than I am, let me tell you.'

Remembering this might be all new to Dame Claire and Frevisse, Luce asked, 'Do you know about Master Knyvet? That he has demon-fits?'

'We were told last night,' Dame Claire answered, nothing like interest showing in her tone, her attention back on her sewing.

Frevisse held back from answering at all, not trusting what might come out if she were not careful. But she still looked out the window. Despite the avid talk around her, all there was to see were two men and a woman walking with a white dog in a spring garden on a fair morning. Part of her knew it was not so simple as that, and part of her very much wished it were, and part of her was unreasonably, seethingly angry at Luce and the others for their chatter over what for Lionel was a nightmare that never ended and inevitably included anyone near to him and anyone who cared about him.

How much did Edeyn care? Frevisse suddenly wondered.

Surprised, she cast through her mind to find from where that particular question had come and then shoved it away, along with her memories of them under the oak tree by the road yesterday noontide and walking beside each other in the rose garden yesterday evening. Edeyn's and Lionel's lives were no concern of hers. He would be in her prayers for a while after she had left Minster Lovell, until thought of him slid away under new matters and familiar ways and there would be the end of it. Or she would remember him, pray for him; but only his name and a thought attached to it would be there, nothing particular about him.

Under Dame Claire's quelling indifference, the talk moved away from Lionel and even Edeyn, back to Luce and her marriage hopes and then on to the likely cost of Burgundian cloth this year and what had been used to dye a thread one of the other women was embroidering with so particularly rich a shade of yellow it was near to gold.

Frevisse took no part in the talk. With a little effort she could make the hemming take all her concentration, fill up her mind past any thought except the necessities of even stitches and leaving no bloody marks from pricked fingers. As Dame Claire tied off her final stitch, Frevisse laboriously finished the smock's hem and, heartily sick of it and afraid she would be offered another something to sew, said, 'It must be near to Sext. Should we go to the chapel, do you think, Dame Claire?'

Dame Claire looked out the window at the bright day and garden from where Lionel and the others had long since gone. 'Better yet the church,' she said. 'We've yet to pay our respects to St Kenelm. We can do that and Sext, too. Would that be all right, do you think?' she asked Luce.

'Oh yes. There's plenty of time until dinner,' Luce cheerfully agreed. 'Did you see there's a gate from the garden into the churchyard?'

Dame Claire said they had noticed it yesterday. 'Is it all right with you, Dame Frevisse?'

So far as Frevisse was concerned it was better, combining the chance to move and the chance to be outside. She managed to temper her answer to murmured agreement but was already to the chamber door while Dame Claire was still showing Luce where she had left off sewing, and she only with effort held herself to wait in the antechamber until Dame Claire joined her. With hands folded into opposite sleeves, heads a little bent, and eyes properly to the ground a few yards ahead of them, they went together into the great hall, down it, and out. Frevisse forced herself to hold back her longer pace to Dame Claire's lesser one and thought she had hidden her mood, but once they were outside, taking the well-gravelled paths toward the church-yard gate, Dame Claire asked, 'Better?'

Annoyed and amused together that she had been so obvious, Frevisse said, 'Better. Thank you.'

'Luce should thank me, too.' There was a small smile in Dame Claire's voice. 'You looked as if you were about to do violence to that hapless smock.'

Frevisse laughed softly, already eased by being out. The paths were dried now from last night's rain and all the garden's shades of green and brightness shone in the morning's light, seeming new-made to the day. The gateway into the churchyard was roofed by a little thatched pentice and the gate was unlocked. Beyond it, the path ran on to the church porch through the peace of the churchyard. By the time they reached the door set deep in its porch, Frevisse was wholly quieted, her mind turned toward prayer.

Every church was different, according to the desires of those who built it, but every one was the same, a place where the distance to God seemed less, the soul's hope more reachable. Inside, this one of Minster Lovell was bright with light from the clerestory windows, and like the manor house, it smelled of newness, of stone not long from the quarry and fresh plastering and paint. Frevisse glimpsed its painted walls, dramatic with tall saints and a Judgement Day with demons, all done in bold colours to catch the eyes of worshippers and remind them of the need for prayer, but she and Dame Claire were drawn along the nave toward the altar and St Kenelm's shrine beyond it. Set high to be seen the length of the nave, elaborately carved from stone and painted in blues, reds, and greens touched here and there with gold, in the sunlight from the clerestory above and the east window beyond, it seemingly glowed with its holiness. Lord Lovell did well by his saint, Frevisse thought.

Her eyes on the shrine, she was halfway along the nave before she realized she and Dame Claire were not alone there. Lionel's back was to them where he knelt on the altar steps but she recognized the dark blue houpelande he had been wearing in the

garden earlier, and for even better confirmation the white dog
Fidelitas lifted her head from where she lay on his spread skirts
to look at them. Frevisse glanced around with unformed expectation of Martyn or Edeyn being somewhere near, but there was
no one else. Beside her Dame Claire put out a hand to her arm,
stopping her, and nodded toward Lionel. They exchanged a look
but did not speak, understanding each other well enough. Lionel
was in such a need of prayer that it would be shame to disturb
him. Crossing themselves, they knelt where they were to make
their own prayers, sharing the prayer book Dame Claire carried
at her belt.

Each of a day's nine Offices was different from the others, and
each changed from day to day according to the season and where
they were in a week, but they were also all the same year in, year
out, and linked by the desire for God and the soul's salvation.
Sext, coming in late morning, was a brief office but Frevisse had
long since learned its value, its reminder in the midst of every
day's bothers of eternity. Today, aware even in her prayers of
Lionel kneeling nearby and the curse he carried with him, she
prayed with more compassion than usual its daily reiteration,
'Confer salutem corporum, Veramque pacem cordium.' Give
health to the body, And true peace to the heart.

Or to the soul. Cordium could mean heart or soul. Or both at
once, she supposed, and that would be very right for Lionel.
Peace to his heart and soul, because there seemed small hope of
it for his tormented body.

He was still in prayer when they finished, but as they rose to
their feet in a soft sound of skirts, Frevisse saw his head lift, his
hand move as he crossed himself, meaning he was done, too.
Already on their feet, they left him but in unspoken agreement
waited in the porch for him. It might have been natural to go on,
but their going on might look too much like avoiding him and so
they stayed. Frevisse wondered how often that was the way of it
for him: people either avoiding him in fear and disgust or else

deliberately seeking his company, to prove they did not fear or despise him. And which of the two did Lionel resent the least?

There was no way to know but she caught his hesitation as he saw them, and the swift glance he swept across their faces that told her he was trying to tell if they knew about him now and what they thought of him if they did. It must always be like that for him, she realized – assessing people in the moment that he met them, judging what they knew and how they were going to be toward him if they knew too much.

She did not think that she reacted at all, except to curtsy with Dame Claire who said for both of them, 'Master Knyvet.'

'My ladies,' he answered, bowing.

It was Fidelitas who made it easier, trotting forward to sniff first at Dame Claire's skirts, then at Frevisse's, waving her plumed curve of tail in approval. Lionel smiled with actual amusement. 'She has opinions,' he said.

'She's assuredly taken to you. What's going to happen when you leave here?' Dame Claire asked.

Fidelitas returned to him and he bent to rub her behind the ears. 'I may have to buy her from Lady Lovell by the look of it.' He did not seem to mind the thought or worry that Lady Lovell might demur; he was probably as sure of her kindness as Frevisse was coming to be.

The path was wide enough they could walk together, Fidelitas ahead of them, back toward the churchyard gate. In the sunlight, Frevisse could see Lionel's face was shadowed with tiredness, dark under his eyes, and there was a bruise on his forehead that had not been there yesterday.

Dame Claire commented on the weather. Lionel agreed it was very fair. He moved a little ahead to open the gate and stand aside for them to go through before him. On the path that skirted the greensward, not far beyond the gateway, Edeyn and Martyn Gravesend were coming toward them in close talk, and something Martyn said made Edeyn laugh in the moment before they realized that Frevisse, Dame Claire and Lionel were there. Edeyn's already happy face brightened with wider smile, her hand going up in greeting as she moved more quickly towards them, calling in her bright voice, 'Lionel! My ladies. Well met! We were coming to warn you it's nigh dinnertime, Lionel.'

They met and all turned toward the house, Frevisse falling back to let Edeyn walk on Lionel's other side from Dame Claire. Martyn, as was proper, stood aside to let them all pass, his low bow sufficient greeting. His face, even more than Lionel's, betrayed he had spent a night that had been worse than merely unrestful, shadowed around his eyes and hollowed below the cheekbones as if part of him had been drained away with effort.

Instead of leaving him to walk a few paces behind her, Frevisse said, 'Walk with me, please you.'

Martyn slightly bowed again and did, but left it to her to make conversation if she chose so that for a little way they went in silence, the light flow of Edeyn's talk about the men's successful hunt and Lady Lovell's return passing back to them.

But their pace was slightly slower than the others so that gradually they were a little further behind and then a little further. That was Martyn's doing and Frevisse let him until they were enough behind that what they said would not be easily overheard. Then she looked at him and he returned her look and said, 'You know about Lionel.' Statement, not question.

'Yes,' she agreed. And after a moment's pause she added, 'Everyone knows.'

'By way of Master Giles.' Again not question but fact, bitterly said.

For perfect accuracy, she answered, 'I heard it from Master Geffers first.'

'Who doubtless had it from Master Giles.'

Frevisse slightly inclined her head in acknowledgment.

Martyn smiled wryly. 'Master Giles has a way of making certain no one is long ignorant of it, wherever we are.'

And not out of kindness either, Frevisse wanted to add, but Martyn already knew that, probably more surely than she did. Instead she said carefully, wanting to see his reaction, 'He says that for their safety people should know, on the chance they're there when Lionel is attacked.'

'The only person in danger when Lionel is attacked is Lionel himself. He's the only one that's ever been harmed in them.'

'Giles said you had.'

'Giles would.' For the first time Martyn's tone betrayed that Giles's dislike of him was fully returned. 'In the worst of the fits Lionel flails. He doesn't know it. He doesn't know anything when one is on him. He loses all control of his body and his mind isn't there. I used to be hit sometimes, until I learned better, but that wasn't deliberate by Lionel, only because I was near, and I've learned how to duck since then. Nobody is in any danger from Lionel, not even by chance, because no one but me is willing to be near him when an attack comes. Lionel has always been the only one who's badly hurt in them.'

'The scar down his face?'

'That's one. Once he broke his arm when it caught under the edge of a bed and he wrenched before I could free him.'

Ahead of them Edeyn turned her face smiling up to Lionel, and his laughter and hers and Dame Claire's mingled clear in the morning air. Momentarily Frevisse wondered if that was another cause for Giles's dislike of his cousin. 'How did you know I knew about Lionel?'

'You'd been in Master Giles's company last night. I didn't suppose he had changed his ways.'

'And that's something Lionel knows, too, I suppose.'

'He knows.'

Frevisse had noticed before how much meaning Martyn was able to put into few words. What it was like to be Lionel, caught not only by his demon but between Martyn and Giles? For he was caught, on every side: by the reality that Giles was his heir and therefore could not be ignored; by the necessities forced on him by his attacks; by his need of Martyn because there was no one else willing to take on the danger of caring for him when an attack came.

'And when people know about him, what then?' she asked.

'What do they do? It varies. Some shun him completely. Those are the simplest to deal with. Others keep company with him, but you can see them hoping, behind their manners, to see an attack come on him. Others try to treat him as if there were nothing untoward about him at all, as if he were like anyone else.'

'And mostly he is,' Frevisse said. 'It's not as if he were constantly possessed.' Not like his cousin Giles whose demon was merely of more subtle sort and therefore worse, in her opinion, because less readily seen and dealt with.

'No,' Martyn agreed. 'He's not constantly possessed.'

There was a weariness in his voice that matched the strained tiredness of his face, and completing what he had left unsaid, Frevisse murmured, 'Except by the fear of what could come on him at any time.'

Martyn's look at her was sharp with appreciation and a hint of smile eased his mouth. 'Except for that. But at least he usually has warning. Sometimes as much as half an hour, usually less but almost always enough for him to go where he won't be seen.'

Like a sick, hurt animal, Frevisse thought.

Ahead of them the others had reached the door and Lionel had stepped aside to bow the women through, smiling at them both as he did. Tall and angular as he was, he was not graceful, and his scarred and long-jawed face missed handsome by several degrees, but there was a warmth to him that, like his cleverness and ready laughter, made it easy to like him, and Frevisse abruptly ached with unexpected pain for a life lived the way Lionel had to live his, shunned by other people, always waiting for the evil to come on him despite everything he had done to be free of it, despite all his prayers. Even given the friendship he had from Martyn and Edeyn, he was very much alone.

Chapter 8

DINNER WAS A loud and pleasant meal in the great hall, a jumble of talk among the morning's hunters who apparently had had a good run and taken sufficient deer for a few days' needs, and everyone else with their own matters to complain of, discuss, or laugh over.

Used to the quiet of St Frideswide's refectory where the only voice at mealtimes was the reader's quietly giving the daily reading, Frevisse listened more than she talked to the knights on either side of her about the hunt until they became absorbed in talking past her to each other and then she gladly stopped talking or listening to them at all.

Dame Claire farther along the table was in steady conversation with the gentlemen on her left side but too far away for Frevisse to hear any of it. She did not much care; it was enough that Dame Claire seemed more herself than she had been for a long while past, and probably from more than last night's good rest and the morning's ease, Frevisse thought. The days away from Domina Alys were the larger part of it, and she deliberately put away from her the worry of what would come when they returned to the priory at the end of their pilgrimage. Let today's goodness suffice and the morrows' evils be dealt with when they had to be.

Instead she occupied herself with ignoring the men beside her and watching everything else around the hall, most particularly noticing at the rightward table just below the dais a young boy and girl she did not remember from last night's meal, both of them well dressed and so assured in their manners and each with a woman in attendance on them that almost surely they were Lady Lovell's own children. Frevisse vaguely recalled that there were four Lovell sons and, she thought, two daughters. She was not sure of their ages but some at least were old enough by now to be already sent to other households to be raised, and likely these two here were the youngest, the boy near eight by the look of him and soon to be sent away, too.

He looked something like his mother, with her colouring and strong oval face. Possibly the girl, brown-haired, her eyes heavy-lidded, was more like her father, but Frevisse had never had occasion to see Lord Lovell and could only guess. At least they were giving their nurses no trouble. Like all else she had seen at Minster Lovell, they were well kept and well mannered.

Further down the hall at the lower tables, John Naylor was still in company with Master Holt the steward. Martyn had joined them, and the talk among them looked good-humoured, judging by their smiles. Father Henry, seated just below the high table but at the far end from herself, was deep in talk with Sire Benedict, both of them intent but seeming to be enjoying themselves. To her regret the Knyvets, though at the high table with her, were at its far end so she could not see them at all. Knowing more about them, it would have been interesting to watch what went on among them and it would have helped to pass the time.

This being the day's main meal, there were more courses than last night, and though dishes were served and withdrawn with swift competence, it all went on far longer than Frevisse's hunger or interest in eating. When it ended at last, she rose and withdrew from the table in a haste that was only barely within the bounds of good manners. Dame Claire might be the better for being away from St Frideswide's, but Frevisse was forced to admit that her own problem of an inclination toward impatient ill temper was not particularly abated.

Unfortunately the realization made her impatient.

Inwardly smiling at her own ridiculousness, she eased toward Dame Claire and they stood aside, with neither duty nor place to go to and both of them a little uncomfortable with it. Her going marked by quick curtsies and bows from those she passed, Lady Lovell left the dais through the door to the small room from where the stairs led up to the solar and the bedchambers beyond. A few other people went that way, including the boy whom Frevisse had noticed earlier, accompanied by a squire instead of his nurse now. She did not see the girl and had lost sight of John Naylor and Father Henry in the general shift of people.

Everyone seemed to be scattering to their afternoon duties, and she found it was aggravating to be caught into a routine familiar to everyone else but unfamiliar and useless to her, used as she was in St Frideswide's of being certain where she should be and what she should be doing through her days.

'She said we'd talk to her this afternoon,' Dame Claire said, perhaps out of the same unease, reminding them both there was a reason for their being here. Her hand went to her belt pouch where she carried the papers concerning the priory's case.

'Luce will come for us. Or someone,' Frevisse agreed. And soon, I hope, she added, even if only to herself.

It was not Luce who came but the squire she had seen with the boy. He came back through the door and directly to her and Dame Claire, now alone on the dais except for the servants clearing the tables away. He bowed and said, 'My lady asks you to come to her now, if you will.'

Frevisse had supposed they would go to the garden or parlour until she had seen which way Lady Lovell went. Now she expected they would go up to the solar, but the man led them through the small chamber not to the stairs but to another door standing open on its far side. He went through, bowed deeply, and turned to step out of their away, gesturing for them to enter.

There was no doubting that the room they came into was where the manor's business was done. Or, more likely, the business of all the Lovell lordship. A wide table dominated the room's centre, with record rolls laid out on it, some held open with small lead bars, others labelled and waiting to hand. Two clerks' desks set to one side caught the light across them from the wide window looking out on the yard, and around the walls were chests and aumbrays for the keeping of documents and records as an open door in one of the aumbrays showed. By marriages, royal grants, and purchase, Lord Lovell held properties in more counties of England than he could visit in a year, and here was where the records of all of them were kept.

Two clerks sat at the desks, one copying a draft onto a bright new parchment, the other comparing two documents and making notes on a scrap of paper. Lady Lovell stood beyond the table, still dressed in her green gown, her hand resting on an unrolled scroll as she pointed something out to the boy who had been in the great hall at dinner. She glanced up as they came in and smiled a greeting but went on explaining to him about the number of sheep a particular manor could be expected to graze. 'If more are noted, then either new land has been assarted and there should be record of it, or else they're scanting their fields and the bailiff had best have good reason why. You see?'

The boy's likeness to her was even more marked when they were together. He was dressed simply, in doublet and hose and leather shoes, and had a boy's look of being ready to be gone about more interesting business the moment he might be dismissed, but he said sensibly enough, 'What if the bailiff doesn't have good reason?'

'Then your steward there had better have looked into it and settled the matter long before you begin to go over the figures for yourself and ask him about it.'

'But if the steward is going to see to it, why do I have to know?'

'Because your steward works for you and it's your business to know what and how he does. You're no better than the bailiff who misuses the land if you don't know how well or ill your steward does his duty.'

'And if he doesn't do his duty?'

There was more impudence than honest curiosity in that. His mother, smiling, tapped him lightly on the end of his nose and answered, 'Then like you, he's put to his lessons again until he understands them and does them right. Or more likely, since he's old enough to have learned them if he's ever going to and he seemingly hasn't, we put him out of our service.'

The boy grinned up at her. She put her hand on his shoulder and nodded toward Frevisse and Dame Claire. 'Now here's another matter of business for us. These ladies are from St Frideswide's Priory beside our village Prior Byfield near Banbury. You remember where Banbury is?'

'North of Oxford,' he answered promptly, plainly pleased with himself.

His mother bent a stern look on him. '"North of Oxford" covers much of England. More precisely, please you.'

He scrunched his face with thinking and said, 'It's two days' ride toward Coventry. We went that way when we went to the plays!'

'Exactly,' his mother agreed, letting her pleasure with him show. 'Now, greet Dame Claire and Dame Frevisse, please you.' To them she said in way of formal greeting, 'My youngest son, Henry. Harry,' she added with a smile to show that was what he was mostly called.

Dame Claire and Frevisse curtsied to him and he bowed.

'They're here,' Lady Lovell said, 'because of a dispute over the well at Prior Byfield that our stewards could not settle.'

Dame Claire had taken the papers out of her belt pouch and

now moved forward to hand them to Lady Lovell. 'This is a copy of what's written in our customal concerning the well. Our prioress thought that if you saw it, it would clarify matters for you.'

'Better than my own steward has?'

It was a simple question, not a demand, and there was hint of a smile behind it. Dame Claire answered with that same hint, 'Our prioress thought that perhaps your steward would represent his side more strongly than ours to you.'

Lady Lovell took the paper and said while she broke the seal on it and opened it, 'Your prioress is said to be a contentious woman.'

Dame Claire glanced back at Frevisse, wordlessly asking for help. It would be all too easy to say too much about Domina Alys, little of it to Domina Alys's good, in response to Lady Lovell's comment; and while it was ill to speak against your prioress inside the priory to other nuns who knew her well, it was far worse to speak ill of her outside it and to strangers. But lying was not an honourable possibility either, and since Dame Claire by choice was straight-spoken, she was caught which way to go, and let Frevisse know she wanted her help in answering discreetly what she should not answer directly. Frevisse, who had stayed near the door, willing to keep out of whatever passed between Dame Claire and Lady Lovell in the business because she had been given no authority to do otherwise, gathered her wits and answered with almost no perceptible pause, 'Our prioress is ... somewhat strong in her opinions.'

'And I'm to take her opinion over that of my own man?'

'Not her opinion, my lady,' Frevisse said, coming forward, 'but the witness of the customal where the priory's rights and duties have been laid out since St Frideswide's was founded.'

'Wasn't this brought to my steward's attention?'

'It was,' Dame Claire said. She had been witness to that.

'And he did not see it as you do? As your prioress does?' She did not ask it ungraciously. She was merely questioning on what grounds they challenged her own man.

With equal politeness Frevisse said, 'He serves your interests well, my lady, and so possibly he sees the matter with a partiality he cannot help.'

'And won't I be likely to look at it with the same partiality?'

'He is answerable to you, but you're answerable to no one except God.'

'And my lord husband.'

'And your lord husband,' Frevisse agreed, but added with a respectful inclination of her head, 'who is as one with you in all such matters.'

Lady Lovell fought the beginning of a smile. She and Frevisse were both in earnest over the matter, but that smile told Frevisse that Lady Lovell was enjoying their play of words and wits as much as she was. Matching the respectful inclination of Frevisse's head, Lady Lovell agreed, 'We are as one.'

'So if you defraud the priory knowingly,' Frevisse went on, 'then you would be defrauding yourself – and your lord husband – of God's esteem, and that you would never willingly do. Therefore you're more likely to judge the matter with less partiality than your steward who only serves you. And if even then it seems to you that you have the right in the matter, you may decide to take the cost of the new well on yourself anyway, out of charity to a poor and struggling house of nuns who will in gratitude make many prayers for you, your husband, and your children.'

That last was afterthought, but in Frevisse's opinion there was something to be said on both sides of the argument, despite Domina Alys's refusal to see it, and an offer to balance the matter a little more the nunnery's way made sense. But prayers were not something lightly offered on the nunnery's behalf, nor had Domina Alys said that they could do so, and Dame Claire exclaimed in protest, 'Dame Frevisse!'

Lady Lovell laughed openly, with sympathy as much as amusement, at Dame Claire's protest and – understanding Frevisse had over-stepped in making her offer – at her boldness.

Since she was already in further than she had meant to be, Frevisse suggested, 'You might talk with John Naylor, too, the young man travelling with us. His uncle is the priory's steward, and John works with him and very likely knows what's passed between our man and yours in more detail than we do.'

Lady Lovell nodded. 'I'll do that, too. And then we can talk again. Tomorrow probably, given what I have left to do today.' She moved her hand to indicate the rolls across the table. 'With my husband gone, these are all mine to deal with.' It was plainly something she was used to and did not in the slightest mind. 'Pray you, enjoy yourselves here the while and welcome.'

That was gracious dismissal and they took it as such, curtsying to her with thanks and withdrawing. The squire had waited by the door and, as he stood aside to see them out, Lady Lovell said to him, 'I'd like to talk with Master Knyvet next. He's likely in his chamber or the garden.'

The squire bowed, followed them out, and saw them back to the great hall. After he had left them, they stood uncertain what they should do next, and Dame Claire said tentatively, feeling out the thought, 'I think I should like to go lie down and rest a while.'

Frevisse could see no reason why she should not. Weariness was showing in her face again, the benefit of last night's rest already worn thin, and since they would probably be on the road again tomorrow's morrow, Dame Claire should rest as much as might be now while she had the chance.

Frevisse saw her up the stairs but parted from her in the solar, leaving her to go into the bedchamber on her own while she went on to the chapel. Her purpose was not so much for prayer this time as somewhere to be alone. One was rarely alone in St Frideswide's, but one was not required to be in continual talk there and Frevisse was tired of talk. A while of silence would do as much for her mind and spirit as lying down would hopefully do for Dame Claire's body.

It was briefly a disappointment to find, here as in the church, Lionel yet again before her, kneeling in front of the altar. This time Martyn was with him, kneeling, too, both in prayer. Neither heeded her approach. Only Fidelitas, curled in the folds of Lionel's houpelande where it spread on the floor around him, lifted her head in notice of Frevisse. But Frevisse, mindful that the squire was somewhere looking for Lionel, went forward, careful to scuff her feet a little to let them know she was there, and briefly touched Lionel's shoulder. He turned his head to look at her and she said, 'Lady Lovell has sent someone to seek you but it will likely be a while before he thinks to come here. She wants to talk to you.'

Lionel nodded. 'Thank you.' He pulled at his gown to urge Fidelitas off it and stood up, Martyn with him.

Frevisse wanted to ask, 'How is it with you?' because their drawn faces told that their prayers had not eased them the way her own so often did her, but she held her curiosity in check, made a small curtsy to Lionel's slight bow and Martyn's deeper one, and as they left, knelt herself before the altar.

The departing quick click of Fidelitas's nails marked their going. Frevisse prayed briefly, but God knew as surely as she did that the real reason she had come here was to be alone.

But even alone, with time to look at her thoughts, she could not immediately identify the discomfort that had been increasing in her. She had been aware of it but without time to think about it enough to give it a name. Now she had the time to think about it and in a while discovered – disconcertingly – that she had to call it homesickness.

She shied from that, wanting it to be something else. She did not know what else but not that, not after all her eagerness to be away from Domina Alys and the disharmony growing in St Frideswide's. How could she be aching for somewhere she had so wanted to leave, especially when she was here in so lovely and peaceful a place as Minster Lovell?

She hesitated over the question, probing at it from different ways. St Frideswide's was changed since Domina Edith's death, but in all fairness Frevisse had long since had to admit that was not merely Domina Alys's doing. No matter who had become prioress after Domina Edith, it would have been different, simply because so much of what a priory was depended on its prioress. Frevisse had made herself face that truth early on, when first trying to come to terms with the need for her obedience to Domina Alys. A few times she had thought she had come to those terms and each time found she had not and had gladly taken Dame Claire's reason to be out of Domina Alys's eye and the priory's discomfort because of it. Nor was there any hope the priory would ever change back to the way it had been. Domina Edith was gone.

Frevisse paused to say a prayer for the late prioress's soul. A strong, good, loving soul whose leaving still ached in Frevisse when she was not careful to keep her mind away from the thought.

But Domina Edith had not been all of St Frideswide's, and neither was Domina Alys. Even under Domina Alys, prayers were still the centre of each day there and the rule of silence mostly held. And the prayers and the silence in which to grow nearer to God had been part of why Frevisse had chosen a nun's life in the beginning. She had chosen to come on this pilgrimage with Dame Claire to be out and away from Domina Alys, not to escape St Frideswide's itself, and now she was finding that she wanted to be back there more than she wanted to be away from her prioress.

The realization startled her. She pushed at it but could not make it change. It was the truth. A truth, she told herself mockingly, that she had best remember when she was indeed back in St Frideswide's and faced again with Domina Alys.

Chapter 9

THE MORNING'S HUNT had been good pastime, but the afternoon had dawdled away in idle talk and nothing much to do. Now they were come to evening, with supper finished. Lady Lovell had chosen to spend the last while of daylight in the garden. Her untoward amount of influence with her husband made worthwhile the effort to have her good opinion, and so Giles was come out with the rest, to make show of enjoying himself over the hidden writhe of his impatience. Sharing a cushion with Edeyn on the grass under the trees among those who had chosen to sit with Lady Lovell rather than walk around the garden, he joined in the talk as much as need be. It was mostly idle chat about this morning's hunt, the perfect weather, the evening's beauty, but he made shift to be part of it, and for good measure paid Edeyn particular heed, holding her hand, occasionally sharing a smile with her, even troubling to seem to care what she said, enough to show how much affection there was between them, because Lady Lovell was fond of her and would think the better of him for it.

But it was actually Lionel whom he was most carefully noticing. So far it was going well. The day was this far gone and he had not yet given any sign the next attack was near. It would be soon but had not happened yet, and that was exactly as Giles needed it to be.

That need had ridden him all day. Every hour Lionel passed untouched meant his demon's return was that much nearer, and every hour of waiting meant the chance was greater that it would come where and when Giles wanted it. He had gone on the hunt this morning because if the attack had come then, it would not have served his purpose, and he might as well enjoy himself otherwise. And likewise through the afternoon, he had forced himself to keep clear of Lionel because the attack coming then would have been no use to him either. He had spent the time in the mews discussing hawks, in the stable discussing horses, in the yard watching the builders at their work and considering what changes he would make at Knyvet when it was his; and all the while he had been at pains not to show he was on edge with constantly wondering how Lionel did. He had even prayed to St Michael in his need, because who was more likely to be against whatever demon came to Lionel than the archangel who had fought the Devil himself out of Heaven?

For good measure he had thrown in promise of a gift rich enough to turn even an archangel's head if this went the way he wanted it to, but still been hugely relieved to see Lionel still upright and competent at supper.

Since then, with time now running close, it was difficult not to watch him obviously and, damn him, he was making it no easier with his pacing around the garden instead of sitting decently still somewhere. Not that it mattered. There was no way he could leave the garden without Giles seeing him go, or someone else who would then undoubtedly comment on it. Most likely Edeyn.

Giles was finding that watching her watch Lionel while trying to seem that she was not was somewhat less amusing than usual. Her glance went Lionel's way rather too often. It was no more than her idiot sympathy for every sick, hurt thing that came her way, and Lionel was the most deeply sick, hurt thing she was ever likely to encounter. Besides, she knew as well as Giles did that another attack was near. But her concern was annoying anyway. Fondling her hand, Giles twisted a little hard at her smallest finger, making her gaze flinch around from Lionel standing at the arched way into the rose garden with the nuns to him instead.

She was always somewhat startled when he hurt her; it added to her charm. He kissed the offended finger, smiling to show he had not meant it. She smiled back, believing him, and he regretted he would have to postpone the pleasure of her tonight until after his other – he considered the word and decided it was the right one – pleasures.

Edeyn turned to answer a question from Lady Lovell. Giles turned back to watching Lionel act out his pretence that he had a life beyond his disease. Even now he kept it up, when he was waiting in sure knowledge of how near his demon was.

A few more hours, Giles promised silently. Wait it out a few more hours and then there'll be an end to the pretending and everything made better.

The spring day's mild warmth was turning toward coolness even before the sun was gone. The women and men not sitting with Lady Lovell among the birch trees walked along the paths among the formal garden beds, or in and out the arbour along the rose garden, and sometimes across the grass to join in the talk there, familiar among themselves, their voices light and drifting on the evening air. At garden's end the manor house rose up, its cream-gold walls and stone-traceried windows glowing in the long slant of setting sunlight.

Frevisse and Dame Claire walked together with nothing in particular to say to anyone or even to each other, aware how their quietness and black habits and plain, heavy veils so obviously put them apart from everyone around them. The bright-gowned women, the older ones with their soft veils lifting, drifting, floating lightly as they moved, the young girls with their soft hair falling loose almost always to at least their waists; the men so sure in their laughter and their talk.

Watching them, Frevisse found she was smiling at how

completely they belonged here, now, in this garden, set jewel-like in the surround of sun-warmed manor walls, gracious with laughter and light talk.

'Do you ever wish—?' Dame Claire began, and stopped, which was unlike her, usually so certain of words or else, with equal certainty, silent. Frevisse looked at her questioningly. Dame Claire met her look, smiled, and remade the question. 'Have you ever thought this – or something like it – could have been our life if we had chosen differently?'

Frevisse had thought it. Though there would have been nothing so grand as this for her, her birth and dowry both insufficient for her to marry so high or richly, there could have been something like this, something her own as nothing was or now ever would be, her nun's vows long since taken. Assuredly she had thought of it. But she had also thought of how it was a loveliness that would pass, as all the world's loveliness passed, and though its beauty was in some ways the more precious for its brevity, it was not more precious than what she had chosen in its stead, and she said with a certainty too great to need emphasis, 'No. I made the choice I should have made. And so did you.'

Dame Claire answered her with an unshadowed smile. 'I know. I only wondered if you did.'

Briefly intent on their own conversation, they had paused beside the arched way into the arboured walk. Now behind Frevisse, Lionel said, 'My ladies, may I join you?' and she turned to find him coming toward them, Fidelitas beside him but no one else.

'Join us and be welcome,' Dame Claire said readily. 'We were going into the rose garden.'

Frevisse had not known they were but went willingly, saying, 'I'm having little luck with my rose allegory,' referring to their yesterday's talk of the poem and its possible meanings. 'Despite myself, worldly ways creep into my mind whenever I'm in the garden.'

'The same trouble Adam and Eve had, I believe,' Lionel said.

They laughed, and Dame Claire bent to stroke Fidelitas's pretty head. 'We thought we might say Compline while we walked but I fear Dame Frevisse keeps humming the cuckoo song.'

'Once!' Frevisse protested.

'The cuckoo song?' Lionel asked.

Frevisse hummed the bright, glad notes of 'Summer is a-coming in, Loudly sing, cuckoo. Grows the seed and blows the mead, And springs the wood anew—'

Lionel grinned. The smile warmed his long-jawed face, and Frevisse realized he *had* been worried how they would be with him. He confessed, still smiling, 'I meant to say Compline, too, but what has been in my head instead is....' He sang, his voice surprisingly light and sure, '"When spray begins to spring, Little bird has her will on her branch to sing."'

'"And I live in love longing for the fairest of all things,"' Dame Claire went on, sure of words and tune.

'You are neither of you to be commended for your piety,' Frevisse said in mock horror.

'But doesn't God accept a merry heart rejoicing in the beauty of his world as worship?' Lionel asked.

'And after all,' Dame Claire added, 'what everyone means when they sing that is that Christ is the fairest of all things and they're longing for Him.'

'Oh, yes, of course that's what everyone means,' Frevisse agreed with over earnest solemnity, and they all three laughed together.

There was nothing uneasy in the silence among them then as they walked on. Fidelitas romped away to see to a beetle crossing the path ahead of them but it flew off ponderously, bumping her nose as it went, and she came back to Lionel's side, eagerly lifting her head to him to be petted. He obliged her.

Frevisse asked, the question coming more easily than it would have before they laughed together, 'Of all the shrines of saints there are, why are you going to St Kenelm's in particular?'

Lionel's look went from her to Dame Claire and back again, and she thought he was judging how they would take him directly talking of his curse, but at the same time his brief smile was appreciative of her directness, and his answer matched it. 'Why Kenelm? Because I've tried so many of the others to no avail. St Margaret of course. St Peter. St Madron in Cornwall. St Giles.' Lionel smiled a little bitterly at the irony of that. 'Even so far afield as St Dympna in Flanders as my need for hope widened. All to no noticeable avail.'

'And why Kenelm now?' A child saint martyred for his goodness in the face of his sister's ambitions seemed an odd choice.

Lionel's gaze on the path ahead of them went distant, to somewhere no one could see who did not live as Lionel was forced to live. And from far inside that somewhere he answered, more to his own heart than her, 'Because St Kenelm surely understands the grief of a life never fully lived. A life ended before it was well begun, the way his was. Maybe out of that understanding, he'll have pity on me. I have no hope in anything any more except holy pity.'

Frevisse wished sharply that she had not asked; but it was Dame Claire who sought to draw him back to them with, 'At least you have a good friend in Martyn Gravesend. A better friend than most men have, no matter what their lives are like.'

'He's my good friend indeed,' Lionel agreed. 'I've been shown that much mercy in my need. Though I doubt my need justifies how much he's let his life be twisted to accommodate my need.'

'Does he see his life as twisted?' Frevisse asked quickly. 'Or does he see it as a choice he freely made and freely holds to?'

Lionel's gaze finally came back from whatever distance or depths he had been seeing. He turned to her, as if facing her would help her more clearly understand his answer and he needed her to understand it. 'He made his choice freely, but he made it years ago. Matters change for every man. I'm bound by a necessity I can't be rid of, no matter what I do. Martyn is bound by his choice and that's a thing he can change if he chooses to. But what if he feels it's a choice he cannot make?'

'Do you want him to?'

'No. For my own sake I don't want him to. But for his sake I've told him that he can.'

'And he says?'

'He says he wants no change.'

'But you don't believe him.'

The lines down Lionel's face beside his mouth that were too old for his years deepened. 'If I had the chance and choice, I'd be as far away from the life he lives as I could possibly go. It's hard to accept he stays willingly, given the choice.'

'But you've given him the choice and he's chosen to stay,' Dame Claire said. Her deep voice softened. 'We were talking of choice just now, Dame Frevisse and I. Even knowing how different, how much more comfortable our lives might have been if we'd chosen otherwise, we still hold whole-heartedly to the choice we've made. It may be that way with him.'

'He's maybe done what so few people do,' Frevisse said. 'He's knowingly chosen a duty that matters more to him than what other people would see as pleasures. He's maybe accepted what's so rarely accepted by anyone despite all Christ's teachings. That we're all responsible for one another. If not for each other's actual souls, then at least for each other's bodily well-being, to do what we can so that souls aren't corrupted by our bodies' miseries.'

'Our bodies' miseries,' Lionel echoed. Frevisse inwardly flinched. Caught up in working through her thought, she had forgotten that the body's misery was something more horribly real to Lionel than mere words.

Edeyn's bright voice interrupted, calling from the arbour entrance, 'Lionel! My ladies! I've come to warn you we're going in.'

Frevisse's gaze was on Lionel's face in the moment that Edeyn called, and she saw the momentary, unthinking pleasure there as he lifted his head and turned toward his cousin-in-law, a pleasure instantly buried behind an everyday smile and answering wave back to her as he casually called, 'We're coming.'

But Frevisse had seen enough, that taken together with what she had earlier observed, she could guess that here was another grief cutting at Lionel's heart. The grief of love where there should not be love. A love without hope. And she wondered, with aching pity, how long he had hurt with that as well as all his other pain – and wondered, too, how sick to his soul he was of other people's pity.

Chapter 10

HEY WERE FINALLY come back to their chamber, the evening
finished, the shutters closed over the window against the bane
of night air. The room had not been meant for three people to
share at once along with their servants and now that damned
bitch for bad measure. If they all moved at once, they were in
each other's way more than they were out of it, but of course and
inevitably Lionel had to be seen to first, the rest of them shoved
aside the while.

Just now, for once, that suited Giles well enough. Sitting on a
chest against the wall near the door, one leg drawn up to cross
his arms on as he waited, he watched while Lionel was changed
from his best gown to a rougher doublet, the servants seeing to
warm water for him to wash face and hands in, bringing a clean
towel for him, taking his belt and dagger to put away until
tomorrow, waiting with his other shoes; Martyn changing, too,
into a more serviceable doublet to see him through what was
coming, all of them like so many idiot ants, not a full brain
among them if they were all added together, not one of them
able to make the smallest guess toward how useless everything
they were doing was.

The lamps' light had shoved the shadows back into the
curtained depth of the bed and the room's corners, so he had to
control his face at that thought. It had brought laughter too close
to the surface. He shivered a little, with nervousness, not fear,

the nervousness of eagerness, and he enjoyed the feeling. What he wanted was so near now. All he had to do was wait while these fools went their fools' ways, just as they always did when they knew an attack would come soon. See Lionel into rough clothing that would not come to grief with his grovelling on the floor. Send him and Martyn off to whatever church or chapel was to hand. Leave them to pray for Lionel to be spared this time.

How long had Lionel been doing this, and still he could not grasp it was going to do him no good? He prayed and he prayed, and over and over, his prayers were ignored. Every time his demon came and was probably as amused by now as Giles was at Lionel's useless attempts to be rid of it. Lionel was a fool. He'd be taken as he was always taken and sprawl out on the chapel floor with his grunting and spittle until it was over, when he could just as well go to bed and let it take him in comfort and more conveniently.

But where would be the glory for Martyn in that? No, Lionel would go to the chapel and Martyn would go with him and they would kneel together, making their pointless prayers, and then Lionel would convulse and Martyn would tend to him, and afterward Lionel would be grateful and Martyn, the arrogant bastard, would go on living off of him.

Only, after tonight, he wouldn't.

Giles rocked slightly back and forth, containing his pleasure with difficulty, because tonight was going to be different. A little while longer, that's all he had to wait, and then things were going to be very different. Finally.

To give his tension some release he said at random, 'I saw that stable oaf Petir today.'

Lionel turned from the servant who had been fastening up his doublet and asked, 'Petir?'

From the side of his eyes, not seeming to, Giles watched Edeyn and Martyn's reactions more than Lionel's. They were more likely to be the amusing ones since Lionel had never understood anything about Petir. Edeyn looked up from where she was sitting on the window seat, heeding him but going on stroking that damned white bitch that fawned on her almost as much as it did on Lionel. Martyn's back was to him, picking up Lionel's cloak from a stool.

'The fellow you had to turn away last year or so,' Giles said to Lionel. 'He's back in the stables here.'

Still nothing from Edeyn, but Martyn, feigning more concern at folding Lionel's cloak over his arm than in Petir, said, as if it were a minor matter, 'He came to us at Mistress Edeyn's marriage but wasn't satisfied and so came back to Minster Lovell.'

Lionel nodded vaguely, probably still not remembering anything at all about the man and his mind on other things. It was Edeyn who asked, 'How goes it with him?'

'Right enough so far as I could tell.' With a slight edge, Giles added, 'I didn't make occasion to talk to him,' reminding her that he had not forgotten the reason he had forced Martyn to send the man away.

If she flushed, there was too little light to see it. Not that it mattered except as momentary diversion. There had been nothing on her part except simple-witted flattery at a stable scruff's admiration. Giles had made her understand the unsuitability of being pleased by that with hard talk and some heavy bed-play and seen to Martyn sending the oaf away. Except he had happened to see him today, he would not have bothered with thought of him again, or bothered with mention of him except for his own diversion, to see himself through this fussing time Lionel and Martyn were so pointlessly indulging in.

The bitch stirred under Edeyn's hand, rose to its feet, and began to whine at Lionel. Edeyn tried to quiet it, but it had lost interest in her and left her to go across to Lionel where he sat on the bed edge changing from his good leather shoes to cloth ones whose toes would not scuff on the chapel floor while he knelt.

The bitch ran its head in under his arm, nosing into his hold, whining more insistently, and he paused to stroke its head, a hand cupped under its chin while he asked, 'What's the matter, girl? Are you ready to leave us? Tired of us?'

The bitch pushed against him harder, whining up into his face as if in real distress. Lionel patted her but rose, ready to go.

'Edeyn, see to her, won't you?'

Edeyn went to him, but the bitch did not want to be held. It tried to follow as Lionel moved away toward the door, and Edeyn knelt and wrapped her arms around its neck. It ignored her, whining more.

'It'll bite you,' Giles said without moving to help her.

No one heeded him. Martyn had opened the chamber door, was standing aside for Lionel to pass. Lionel turned in the doorway to look back. At the bitch? At Edeyn? Giles was not sure and had the thought that it was two bitches together, both looking at Lionel with matching expressions of distress, hurt, and worry.

For a moment Giles thought that Lionel was going to answer them, but his cousin shook his head instead, at them or at something in himself, and left. Martyn followed, shutting the door, and the room was suddenly much larger, more at ease.

'You're not taking that bitch to bed with us,' Giles said.

Edeyn did not answer except to stand up, releasing the cur as she did. It went immediately to the shut door, sniffed at its lower edge and up to the handle to be sure there was no way out, whining lightly.

Edeyn nodded at her maidservant, who had been waiting at the room's far end, to come forward and begin readying her for bed. Giles rose for his own man to do the same for him. Tonight, with Lionel gone, the bed was theirs. Last night they had had to make do with the truckle that pulled out from under it because, as always, Lionel had come first. For once the thought brought Giles more amusement than bitterness. There was going to be an end to that now. All he needed was for Lionel to reach the chapel and for there to be time for the household all to settle. Everything else had already been put into his hands. He only needed that little more.

'Put my bed gown there,' he said, pointing at the foot of the bed when he was undressed and ready to lie down.

His man obeyed and then turned down the coverlet and sheets as Edeyn's woman was doing from the other side. Across the room the bitch had given up trying to go out and had lain down, a tight bundle of displeasure, in front of the door. That was a complication Giles did not want. Tersely he said, 'That cur will whine all night if it's left there. Bring it up on the bed, Edeyn.'

She smiled at him, the first gladness she had shown since they came back to the room, and while he lay down, went to scoop up the bitch. As she brought it back with her to the bed, it whimpered but did not resist. But then it wouldn't, would it, given the chance of a bed instead of the floor, Giles thought.

'Not between us,' he said as Edeyn began to push it toward the bed's middle. 'Keep it on your side.'

Edeyn pulled it back and put herself between it and Giles, speaking soothingly to it. For once her attention turned away from him failed to annoy Giles. If anyone chanced to wonder why he did not make use of Edeyn tonight, the bitch there would be reason enough.

The servants drew the curtains around the bed. Giles lay in the shadows, listening while they set the room to rights and then settled on their pallets on the floor. Beside him Edeyn lay with her back to him, still talking to the bitch. It might be well to let her keep it afterwards, if Lady Lovell agreed. It would give her something to weep over until the baby came, a distraction so she would be less inclined to cling to him. Let her cling to the bitch instead.

The light from the single small lamp left to burn through the night shone dimly through the curtains, their woven pattern of vines and leaves showing in dark relief against it. Waiting for

sounds of sleep around him, Giles speculated on how much a full
set of curtains like that might cost. Of course these might have
cost Lord Lovell nothing, if they were plundered out of France.
Much of this place was likely furnished with French takings. He
had had it easy enough, hadn't he? A strong inheritance, a rich
marriage, French plunder. No wonder he could live like this.
Some folk had it harder.

But if you were neither coward or fool, there were ways to
make the luck you were not born to. Giles smiled to himself in
the darkness. Making his own luck was what he meant to do
tonight.

He waited, keeping himself still with an effort. His man slept
first, his light snoring a sure sign he was gone and unlikely to
rouse until kicked awake in the morning. Edeyn's breathing
evened next. Giles felt her slacken next to him and dared rise up
a little to look down at her, still on her side, her arm over the
bitch's back. The little cur itself was awake right enough. Its head
lifted to look back at him, but it made no sound or other movement, and since that was all he wanted from it, he sank back
down to wait the while longer until snorts told him the maidservant was gone deep to sleep, too.

He held himself in check even then, forcing himself to quietness a little more, to be sure of all of them. Then with great care
he slid to his feet and reached to take his bedgown with him. The
bitch raised her head to watch him go but made no sound or
other movement as he slipped from between the bed curtains
into the room.

The servants were rolled into their blankets on their pallets
across the room, well out of his way to the door. He wrapped his
bedgown around his nakedness and took time to sit on a stool to
put on his shoes. The floors were cold enough, he did not want
to risk being chilled to the point of shivering; the shoes, soft-
soled, would make no noise if he walked carefully. He shivered
as he rose but that was from excitement, not cold, and he willed

himself to control it. For just now every emotion had to be kept in close check, until everything had been done and all the matters afterward settled. Then there would be pleasures enough and time to indulge in them.

The chamber door made no sound as he went out and eased it shut behind him. He stood for a moment in the antechamber's darkness, listening, but so far as he could tell, there was no one else stirring. Even from the great hall so near to hand, where most of the Lovell servants bedded for the night, there was no sound. He looked down at the night lamp's thin line of light showing under his own door's edge, the door's thickness all there was between him and safety, bed. Just that, and nothing to stop him going back to them.

Nothing but his intent and his necessity. And for both of those he had will enough to see him through what little had to be done. He realized he was smiling to himself in the darkness and moved cat-footed toward the stairs up to the chapel.

He made no betraying sound as he went. He had taken time that afternoon, when there was no one to notice him, to ascend and descend the stairs twice, to count them and how many paces it was from their head to the chapel door on the likelihood it would be shut, leaving him no light to go by.

He had been right about that, he found. He ascended into darkness but, sure of his going, paused only at the head of the stairs to listen to the slight smother of laughter from behind the door of the priest's room. It was opposite the chapel, and the lamplight at its bottom and low voices from inside meant the two priests – Sire Benedict and the nuns' large oaf – were sitting up late, probably over wafers and wine of better sort than what they gave at the altar. Priests did well for themselves, and house-priests better than most, though if he had been reduced to priesthood, his choice would have been to be a nunnery's priest, with easy living and a plentitude of women to hand.

He silently laughed at himself, standing there thinking about women and priests, for Christ's sake, when he had something better than either to deal with just now.

The chapel door gave to his careful push. He eased in, paused to be sure he was not heeded and that Lionel and Martyn were exactly as he had expected them to be, kneeling at the altar, their backs to him, then closed the door without sound and slid along the wall into the nearest corner's deep shadows.

Lionel was nearer to the altar, Martyn a little behind him and to his left. Lionel's knees must be calloused by now from all his useless praying. And Martyn? Giles grinned to himself. Whatever Martyn had, he was sure to go straight to Hell for his hours spent in this pretence of prayer and for his fawning on a damned man. Straight to Hell.

Even from where he stood, Giles saw the difference in Lionel's stillness when it came as utterly as if the life had gone out of him. In the same moment Martyn raised his head, and in the next, as Lionel's body shuddered and his head jerked back, then forward, Martyn was on his feet, taking hold of him but unable to stop the wild twist of Lionel's body. It crashed them both to the floor and only Martyn's hand ready under Lionel's head saved his skull from a bruising blow. Martyn scrambled into balance on his knees again, not letting go of Lionel, but, mind gone and body thrashing, Lionel writhed and grunted, his legs and arms battering the floor, his head flinging from side to side. Martyn tried to hold him down from the worst of it, praying over him in short, panting bursts while mostly avoiding Lionel's flailing arms.

Giles was momentarily afraid the priests would hear and come, but there were two heavy doors and their own jollity to shield them; and the parlour below the chapel was empty this time of night. Here was as safe from interruption as any place was likely to be. And if it was not meant to happen, why should everything have fallen so readily into place? He would have done it wherever the next chance came, he had reached the end of patience, but with it coming here at Minster Lovell, who would suspect anything because who would do deliberate murder here when there were other, potentially far safer places for it? The only great trouble could have been Lord Lovell, but with him gone, nobody was likely to see anything except the obvious or ask unfortunate questions. Not that Giles meant for there to be anything to question. He was going to make it obvious what had happened, with no need for anyone to question anything. God himself must be sick of Lionel's misery, to have made it all so easy.

And now was coming what he waited for. Lionel's flailing faltered. His body went on jerking as if unable to give it up, his head still twisting from side to side, but the spasming of his legs and arms slackening until at last he was only lying there, sprawled out on his back, drawing breath in deep, raw gasps, still unconscious but finally quiet.

With a heavy sigh, Martyn let loose of him and sank back on his heels. In the usual way of things, he would now spread the cloak over Lionel to keep him warm, try to make that useless husk of a body comfortable, and then wait through the uncertain while until Lionel regained what passed for his wits. After one of these massive attacks that could be until dawn.

But not this time, cur, Giles promised silently. Quiet-footed, quickly, any sound of his movement covered by Lionel's heavy breathing, Giles closed in behind him.

The main problem had been the weapon. Giles had considered it carefully, because it had to stay here. That meant he could not use his own nor bring an unexplained one with him, and Lionel always left his belt and dagger behind when he knew one of these attacks was coming. That left only Martyn's dagger and now, like everything else Giles had needed to be right for tonight, it proved to be no problem at all. Martyn was still crouched beside Lionel's body, leaning forward a little on his hands, head hanging while he recovered himself from the fight against Lionel's madness. Giles's hand slipped along his side from behind and had his dagger out of its sheath before Martyn knew he was there.

He felt it leave the sheath, though, and Giles could have struck then, simply, before Martyn could turn and know who was there, but that was not what he wanted. He wanted Martyn to know who did it to him. He wanted to be the last thing Martyn saw before he went to Hell.

And it was easy. Simply a matter, with Martyn on his knees in front of him, beginning to turn, of reaching around to clamp his free hand across Martyn's forehead and jerk it backwards so that Martyn stared upward into his face, too taken by surprise to resist. Giles, sure and harsh with pleasure, smiled down at him, saw recognition come, and slashed the long edge of the dagger across his throat, high up under the chin, flesh and windpipe gashed open in one clean stroke.

Martyn's expression had hardly begun to change toward surprise when it went blank with shock. His hands moved toward his throat where there was blood now. Giles shoved him forward, away. Martyn lurched, one hand scrabbling outward as if to grab hold of something that would stop the dying, but there was not anything would do that now. His harsh gargling was an attempt to cry out but he had no voice to cry with; blood and breath were rasping out of the wound together. He was dead even while he was trying to live, and Giles in sudden exaltation shoved him again, sending him in a sprawl across Lionel's body, and then stood over him, watching, until all movement and any sound ceased.

It had been so easy.

Chapter 11

THE DAWN DARKNESS was astir with the murmur and movement of women the whole length of the long room. There
was protest at the night lamp being out – 'It was *not* my turn to
be sure it was filled' – and someone set open a shutter at the
room's far end, making a rectangle of lesser darkness that was
small help. Light showed under the edge of Lady Lovell's door
but it was nobody's business to be disturbing her. Whoever had
turn at attending her last night would be seeing to her now; the
rest of them were expected to be readying themselves for the day,
in the dark or otherwise.

After years of midnight and dawn risings in the nunnery,
dressing in the dark was no particular problem for Frevisse and
Dame Claire. They had laid out their outer gowns, wimples, veils,
and shoes ready on either side of the bed when they undressed,
and now while the other women were still complaining and
groping, they put them back on without fuss or fumbling, Frevisse
putting the last pin in her veil when Dame Claire, already
finished, came around the bed to say in a low voice, 'We could go
to the chapel to pray before the household comes.'

Frevisse, realizing that was a thought she should have had
herself instead of indulging in satisfaction at how adroitly she
and Dame Claire were managing compared to the other women,
agreed immediately; it seemed she was in particular need of
prayers. With a quiet word to one of the women near Dame

Claire and by the faint light through the window, they made their way to the door and out into the solar. Its unshuttered window and the growing dawn outside gave light enough; they crossed it without trouble, lengthwise to the door to the chapel's antechamber where the door standing open into the chapel itself let out welcome lamplight. Dame Claire was leading, and it was into her that Father Henry blundered, bursting out of the chapel as she reached the door. They both cried out and so did Frevisse, all of them startled, but Father Henry's cry had the more fear in it, and behind him, from the chapel, Sire Benedict called out shrilly, 'What is it? God have mercy!'

Father Henry had instinctively grabbed Dame Claire by her arms to keep her from falling. Now he hurriedly let her go, broke off the apology he had started, to call back, 'The nuns! It's only the nuns!'

'Keep them out! For God's pity, keep them out!'

Frevisse had no intention of keeping out. Father Henry was easily flustered but not readily made afraid, and he was afraid. Sire Benedict's voice held horror as well as fear, and while Dame Claire recovered her feet from Father Henry's and tried to ask him what was the matter, Frevisse slipped past them both into the chapel.

Two bodies were sprawled on the floor in front of the altar with Sire Benedict poised over them, his hands held out as if he meant to bless them. But his face, turned toward her, held not blessing but the shock and blindness of someone wanting to deny what he had seen.

But Frevisse saw all too clearly. Lionel first, stretched out on his back, his chest heaving as if he were trying to rouse from a heavy sleep, his head beginning to roll a little and his arms to move. Then Martyn out-flung beside him, arms and legs care-lessly thrown wide, his head canted aside so there was no way not to see the red slash high across his throat or the empty gaping of his face.

Frevisse had encountered death before, some as bad as this, but she turned her head away, sickened both by the ugliness and by her memory of Martyn as she had last seen him, laughing. Alive.

Sire Benedict, determined she should not be there, stepped between her and the body, shooing his hands at her, saying in distress, 'It isn't something you should see, my lady, please, go back, this isn't something—'

'I've already seen,' she said. She had only with difficulty learned to keep her vow of obedience after she became a nun, and there were still times, when a matter was urgent enough, that she chose to forgo it. 'We have to take Master Knyvet out of here before he fully rouses.'

Sir Benedict boggled at her, as if that were too difficult a thought for him to manage just now, but behind her Dame Claire said, 'He shouldn't see Martyn like that. Father Henry, help me. Sire Benedict's room, I think.'

As the priory's infirmarian, she was used in her own way to the disasters that could befall a human body, and when there was any chance at all to help or mend she fought fiercely; but there was no hope at all of Martyn and so Lionel was her concern. She went forward in her brisk certainty of what needed to be done, and Frevisse went with her, seeing more clearly what must have happened here.

Lionel was stirring more, closer to consciousness, she guessed. Martyn's blood was matted darkly across him and on the floor beyond him, far more than was on Martyn himself. A practical corner of Frevisse's mind noted that though Martyn lay partly on the woven carpet that ran down the altar steps and across the floor, Lionel was sprawled off of it and all the blood was on him or beyond him, leaving the carpet unmarred. That was the single good thing here, she thought, defending herself against the increasingly sickening realization of what must have happened here, a realization worse than what she actually saw. A bloodied dagger lay on the floor at Lionel's side. Its empty sheath was on Martyn's belt. All the blood was apparently Martyn's. There seemed to be was no wound at all on Lionel.

'It was his demon,' Sire Benedict said behind her. 'In his madness, when his demon came, he killed his man. God have mercy, God have mercy, God have mercy—'

'It's *our* mercy Lionel needs now,' Frevisse snapped. Lionel was too much for her and Dame Claire to handle, even between them. 'Help us,' she demanded. 'He has to be taken out of here.'

'It's the only mercy we can give him,' Dame Claire said. 'He mustn't see his friend like this.'

Her appeal more than Frevisse's demand seemed to reach Sire Benedict and Father Henry both. They came and between them lifted Lionel out of the gore he lay in. Much of the blood went with him, soaked into his clothing, but at least he would be away from sight of what he had done. Dame Claire went ahead to push the chapel door wide and open the way into Sire Benedict's room. She said over her shoulder as she went, 'I'll go and tell Lady Lovell. She has to know as soon as may be.'

Frevisse stayed where she was; it would be wrong to leave Martyn's body alone even for that little while. He had died in violence and without time for the last things that should be done to insure the soul's safe going from the body. He needed prayers, as soon and as many as could be managed.

She tried to gather her wits to it but found she was only looking down at the darkened blood and abandoned dagger, trying to understand what had happened beyond the certainty that Martyn's death had come from Lionel's hand. Not by Lionel's will surely; he must have been possessed when he struck the blow. Not that it mattered, she supposed. The final reality was what they would all have to deal with, more than how or why it had happened.

Sire Benedict returned alone. Past the first horror now but avoiding a direct look at Martyn's body, he said calmly enough,

'Father Henry is staying with Master Knyvet. He's strong enough to restrain him if that's needed.'

'Has he been told? Is he conscious enough to understand?'

'Not yet. He's like someone taking a long while to come out of a heavy, heavy sleep.'

He brought himself to look down at Martyn's body and made the sign of the cross over it, but as he raised his head, he saw the altar and his expression changed as a new realization came on him. 'And everything here is profaned. It may even have to be reconsecrated! Oh, God have mercy!'

His cry was from the heart, and Frevisse silently echoed it. The shedding of blood had made the chapel unholy, unusable. Water and heavy scrubbing would maybe cleanse away the blood but the pollution of spirit would only yield to a complex ritual and until that was done, the place could no longer be used for any sacred services.

Sire Benedict moved past her to the altar, genuflected, took the small gold box of consecrated wafers out of the silver-gilt tabernacle, genuflected again, and extinguished what was meant to be a perpetual flame in the red-glass lamp, sign of the Presence that could not stay here now. Everything holy in the room would have to be taken out, kept elsewhere, until the chapel had been made fit for sacred use again. Frevisse felt the priest's pain with her own.

Beyond the chapel an agonized outcry of grief broke into the dawn quiet. Wrenched by its pain, Frevisse turned toward the open chapel door in helpless answer. Lionel now knew what he had done.

The next moment there was a rouse of voices and clutter of footfalls from the solar and up the stairway. People were coming, more than a few, and Frevisse said, 'Don't let them all come in. Only the ones that are needed.'

Sire Benedict looked at her uncomprehendingly, then understood what she meant and reached the doorway as the first of the on-comers did, barring their way and declaring, 'No, no, it's better you don't come in. Not yet. We want Master Holt. This is for him to deal with. Someone bring Master Holt. Tell him he's needed.'

His authority was enough to hold them back but not stop their questions. Words beat at him and he answered them with what he knew. There was no point in not telling, but beyond him Father Henry's voice rose as he kept back anyone who wanted past him to Lionel in the priest's room.

Frevisse turned her back on the growing press of people and their rising noise. Instead she went and knelt beside Martyn's body, forcing herself to concentrate on his need, praying the first words that came into her mind from the Office of the Dead. *A porte inferi erue, Domine, animas eorum.* From the gate of Hell, Lord, deliver their souls.

Martyn's soul was gone, Lionel's still trapped here on earth, but however it was with Martyn's soul now, Lionel's was all too surely in torment. They were both, both desperately in need.

Pain for their pain burned in her; but even then, beyond the intensity of her prayers, she could not help knowing that Sire Benedict was still holding the doorway and she thought the better of him for it. He was neither a fool nor coward as she had first feared, only a man caught out of his ordinary way of things, and though he had not shifted on the instant to face them, he was managing now. But relief was nonetheless plain in his voice as he cried, 'Master Holt! Thank God! Can you make them go away?'

Master Holt could at least silence them. He made his orders crisp and to the point, and the babble of demands and exclaims fell sharply off so that he came into the chapel backed by what might have passed for a respectful hush, though Frevisse as she rose to her feet saw gawking faces still crowded in the doorway before Master Holt firmly shut the door on them.

His look asked whether Frevisse was help or hindrance or someone he could ignore. To show she could be the latter, she stepped back from the body, leaving it to him. Accepting that, he turned and looked first at Martyn's body, then at the evidence of blood on the floor beyond it and asked, 'That's where Master Knyvet lay?'

Sire Benedict had come a few steps after him. 'Yes. He's in my room now. Father Henry is with him. He's all covered with blood.'

'But unhurt himself?'

Sire Benedict's expression reflected Frevisse's own realization that none of them had thought to see for certain if Lionel was wounded or not. Uncertainly he answered, 'No, no hurt on him, I think. Unless it's very small.'

'So all this blood is Gravesend's and more of it is on Master Knyvet.'

'Yes.'

Master Holt's look returned with no eagerness to Martyn's body. 'That wound is too high in the throat to have spewed blood widely. What happened for there to be so much on Master Knyvet? Gravesend must have fallen across him after he was sliced. But that's not the way they were found. What happened?'

He was asking the question of himself, but it was one that had already stirred in Frevisse's mind. Forgetting she was supposed to have no part in this, she said, 'They fell that way and then Martyn was thrown off by some last spasm of Lionel's body.'

Master Holt nodded agreement without looking away from Martyn. 'That would have to be the way of it,' he agreed. 'And then they lay here all the rest of the night until you and the other priest came to ready the chapel for mass.'

Sire Benedict sighed, nodded. His face showed his sadness at what had happened here but no longer fear or shock; the first horror worn off and practicalities were taking its place. 'Let me put this away,' he said, indicating the gold box with the Host he still held. 'It shouldn't be here longer. Then if you'll have him moved, I'll see to him being prayed over. Lady Lovell has to be consulted as to the morning mass. We can use the church, I suppose. The bishop has to be told as soon as may be.'

'I can send a messenger to him when I send to the crowner to come,' Master Holt said.

'Good, good. I'll write the needed letter.' Sire Benedict's distress was building again, though in a different direction. 'This all has to be cleaned of course. But it won't be right until the bishop has given leave for its ritual cleansing and who knows when that will be? This is all so bad, so very bad.'

Frevisse said quickly, 'Father Henry can help with anything you ask.'

Sire Benedict slightly brightened. 'Of course he can. A good man. Very solid. Oh! I've left him with Master Knyvet this while. Poor man!' Whether he meant Father Henry or Lionel was not clear. 'And there are all those people outside.'

The noise of voices had risen again, maybe even grown, beyond the door. Frevisse could imagine everyone free to come was now crowded into the antechamber, the solar, or on the stairs, hoping for glimpse of something dreadful, of the murderer and the murdered.

'I'll see to them,' Master Holt said grimly, 'and find enough men to view the body while I send the rest away. My lady, you'll come?' he added, making it question rather than order, sure enough that she would be willing to leave.

'No, I'll stay. To pray for him while everything is being sorted out. By your leave, if I may.' She said it as politely as she might; she had no authority here to say what she would do or not do.

But Master Holt accepted without hesitation. 'That would be most good of you.' He had enough to mind that he was willing to take her at the face value she put forward and leave it at that, freeing himself to all the other matters at hand. He made quick work of clearing the gawkers away. Sire Benedict left with his precious burden and Frevisse was alone with Martyn's body and the evidences of death in the chapel, now oddly barren under the extinguished altar light. Dawn had come on enough that there was light in plenty but the sense of holiness was gone and the place was empty without it. Frevisse knelt again beside Martyn's body and for the first time touched it, closing his eyes. The rest she would leave to others, but it would be well if they saw to it soon.

The body was such a useless thing once the soul was gone, but it should have care even then, in honour of when it had been a thing that mattered.

Again words from the Office of the Dead came to her. *Sana me, Domine, quoniam conturbata sunt ossa mea, Et anima mea conturbata est valde....* Heal me, Lord, for my bones are afraid, And my soul is greatly terrified....

They were words apt for Martyn, because in whatever way it had happened between him and Lionel, there must have been at least a moment between disbelief that it was happening at all and death itself for Martyn to be afraid – time for his body's fear as the blow was struck and time for his soul's fear when he realized he was dying. Not long, not with a wound like that across his throat, but time enough. Time for fear and hopefully time for what needed to pass through a man's mind to help his soul toward salvation.

She was too deep into prayer to notice when others came into the chapel until Master Holt said, 'My lady.'

She looked up to find he had brought half a dozen men with him – a few squires and some of the household gentlemen – to see everything there was to see about the body and the place so they could be witnesses at the inquest the coroner would hold when he came. And Lionel's cousin Giles was with them.

He had circled well aside from the others, to where he had a clearer view of the body and the blood. Frevisse took only a glimpse at him, but that was enough for her to want no more. If she had thought about it beforehand, she would not have expected any grief from him for Martyn's death. His dislike of Martyn had been too marked. But that he should so clearly let his gloating show....

Avoiding looking at him again, she rose to her feet, for the first time thinking beyond the present fact of Martyn's death to what it was going to mean to everyone of whose lives he had been part. Plainly Master Giles was ahead of her there, as well he might be, being Lionel's heir, but she did not think she wanted to know his thoughts.

'Lady Lovell has asked you come to her, if it please you,' Master Holt said. 'There's nothing more for you to do here.'

He held out a hand to help her rise and Frevisse took it. There was nothing else to be done here that could not be done as well or better by others, nor had she any particular desire to stay. 'Where is she?'

'In her parlour. The other nun is with her.'

'And Father Henry?'

'I think he's still with Master Knyvet.'

'In Sire Benedict's room?'

'He's been moved to somewhere more secure. For now,' Master Holt said in a limiting voice, answering her and telling her she had asked enough.

She accepted that. He had more to deal with than a nun's questions, and she could guess the rest without him saying it: Lionel was locked away and would be kept locked away until matters were a little more in hand and he could be turned over to the sheriff.

Frevisse slightly bowed her head to him in thanks and left.

The antechamber was empty except for two uneasy men there as some sort of guard against the idly curious coming back.

'Is it bad in there, my lady?' one of them asked her, with a jerk of his head toward the chapel door.

Frevisse nearly said tartly that that depended on how bad you found death and blood, but she caught the thought back before it became words. The man was no more than as curious as she would have been. 'It's bad,' she said quietly and went on, down the stairs to the parlour.

Chapter 12

AT THE FOOT of the stairs from the chapel, the door to the Knyvets' chamber stood partly open. Frevisse had glimpse of a scattering of clothes over the open edge of a travelling trunk that showed there had been haste in dressing, and somewhere inside, out of sight, a woman was crying. While she tried to guess whether it was Edeyn or not, she turned aside to the parlour door where one of Lady Lovell's women hurriedly opened it and made gesture for her to enter.

Her question about Edeyn was answered as she did, for Lady Lovell and Dame Claire were standing at the room's centre and Edeyn was with them, the white dog Fidelitas in her arms and her voice rising, '... couldn't have, never would have! Not to Martyn. Not to *anyone*!'

'We know he didn't,' Dame Claire said, meaning to soothe. 'The demon when it took him—'

'It doesn't take him that way! It *never* has!'

'This time it did,' Lady Lovell said, all the brightness that had seemed essentially part of her gone from face and voice. There was no place for brightness in what had happened, but the strength that had underlain it was to the fore now, and the kindness. But it was a kindness of the sort that would not yield the reality of fact, even to ease pain as great as Edeyn's. 'Look you, Edeyn, Dame Frevisse is come. Let her tell us what she saw.'

Edeyn's expression as she swung around on Frevisse was a

mixture of challenge and despair, and both were in her voice as she demanded, 'What more is there beyond what Dame Claire already told us? What else is there to know if you don't believe me?'

Calm with the assurance of authority, Lady Lovell answered evenly, 'I prefer a belief built on facts, not feelings. We've heard Dame Claire. Now I want to hear Dame Frevisse. Later I'll hear Sire Benedict and the other priest, and Master Holt when he's seen to all that needs seeing to.'

'But you won't hear me!' Edeyn cried.

'I've heard you. And I'll hear more if you have more to tell, the way I'll hear everyone who has anything to say to the purpose about it before I'm done.' Because in her husband's absence the matter was hers to deal with until the crowner – the royal officer summoned in any matter of unnatural death – could come. She was bound by law to do it, and the more that she could tell him, the less trouble he would have in reaching a decision over the cause of death and what should be done because of it.

And the sooner that was done, Frevisse thought, and everything understood, the sooner Edeyn could begin to accept it. In the meanwhile facts faced now would be kinder to her than her raw emotions.

The same thought was maybe in Lady Lovell's mind as she laid a hand on Edeyn's arm and said in gentle command, 'Edeyn, just listen.'

Edeyn held momentarily rigid in face and body, near to refusing anything asked of her with an anger and a grief and a strength of stubbornness Frevisse had not suspected in her. But defiance was too unfamiliar to her, obedience too usual, and with an angry gasp that was halfway to tears, she gave way, sank down on the cushioned bench, and pressed her face against Fidelitas's neck like a small child forced to endure something she would rather escape.

Lady Lovell turned her gaze to Frevisse and said with the simple expectation of being obeyed, 'My lady, tell us what you saw.'

Frevisse bent her head in acceptance of the request and acknowledgement of Lady Lovell's right to ask it, then steadily, with as little emotion as possible, told what she had seen in the chapel, from encountering Father Henry in the doorway and his first words through to leaving Martyn's body to Master Holt. Though she kept her gaze on Lady Lovell while she talked, she was aware of Edeyn while she did, aware that she sat without movement or sound, her arms tight around Fidelitas, her face hidden. Nor did she look up when Frevisse had finished.

Lady Lovell said sadly, 'That's as Dame Claire told it and I expect no different from Sire Benedict and your priest. The dagger beside Lionel's hand, was it surely Martyn's dagger?'

'I don't know for certain, only that it was there and Martyn's sheath was empty,' Frevisse answered.

'Someone will be able to identify it, surely and for certain, but there's no great doubt, is there? Edeyn, do you see how it must have been?'

Her face still hidden against Fidelitas, Edeyn nodded.

'And I can tell you for certain it is Martyn's dagger,' Giles said from the doorway. The door had not been quite closed, and he had stood there long enough to hear what the nun had had to say before he nudged it wider to see there were only women there. The woman who was probably supposed to have seen it shut and kept that way was turned away from it, listening as hard as the rest of them to every detail the nun had to tell.

So much for any claim that women were more tender than men.

He had chosen his moment to speak and enjoyed the startled turn of heads and even more the way Edeyn looked up, gasped with relief, and put the bitch aside to rise and come to him, wanting his arms for comfort. He took her willingly, held her close, and said over her head to the others, 'There's no doubt it's Martyn's dagger. I saw it myself just now.'

'And Lionel's dagger?' Lady Lovell asked. 'It wasn't drawn at all?'

'Lionel never went armed when he knew one of his attacks was coming,' Giles said. 'He knew it wasn't safe.'

Edeyn drew a little away from him. 'But it wasn't because anyone was afraid he'd use it, only that if he fell on it, he'd likely be hurt. He has to be kept from falling against things, on things, when the fit takes him. He never hurts anyone.'

'Edeyn,' Giles said, still holding her close, 'this time he did. Martyn is dead.'

He felt her flinch from that and tightened his hold on her, saying with a tenderness he almost felt, 'Gently, dear heart, gently. Remember the baby. That's who you have to care about now. And yourself. Martyn is dead. Lionel killed him. That's something we have to live with from now forward.'

Edeyn made a small twisting movement, as if to pull free, but he kept her close to him and whispered, 'The baby, Edeyn. Think of our child.'

She subsided, leaning her head against his shoulder before asking in a hushed voice, 'What will happen to him?'

Meaning it less for her than for Lady Lovell, Giles said, 'You have to understand that it wasn't simply murder. Lionel was out of his right wits when he killed Martyn and so things are better than they might be.'

'Better!' Edeyn said resentfully, refusing the thought.

'If it had been plain murder, everything Lionel owns would be forfeit to the king. But he wasn't sane and so everything will be kept in ward against the chance he comes into his right mind again.'

He glanced at Lady Lovell to see how much of that she had understood, but Edeyn cut off any answer the woman might have made with, 'But he is in his right mind again! Always when the attack ends, he's himself again!' She twisted around in his arms to make her plea to Lady Lovell. 'Is that what the law says? That if he recovers from madness, then he's free?'

'But he isn't recovered!' Giles said sharply, jerking her back to face him. He had not expected her to understand it easily, but her blind focus on Lionel was beginning to anger him. 'He'll never be recovered. His demon can come on him again any time. He'll never be free of it, and so long as he isn't, he's dangerous!'

'He's not!'

'Edeyn,' Lady Lovell said with something more than gentleness, demanding to be listened to, 'your husband has the right of it.'

Giles kept the surge of triumph from his face. If the woman had that much of the law in her head, then he was well on toward the next step of what he meant to make out of Martyn's death. Gentle again, he said, 'Edeyn, love, you have to understand what's possible and what isn't.' He looked pleadingly toward Lady Lovell. 'Help me make her see.'

As he had hoped, Lady Lovell came to take Edeyn from him, to lead her away to the cushioned bench and sit beside her while she explained, 'Edeyn, we know it wasn't Lionel who killed Martyn. Not in the strictest sense. No one believes Lionel had any will to Martyn's death. His demon had him when it happened, surely. But he did strike the blow. It came from his hand.' Her hold on Edeyn's hands tightened. 'No, listen to me. He won't be executed for it, but he can't ever be free while the likelihood of it happening again is still with him.'

'And it's going to be with him always,' Edeyn said. 'So he'll be locked away for always, for something he never did. That isn't fair.'

'No more than Martyn's death is fair,' Lady Lovell returned. 'There's no fairness in this anywhere. All we can do is keep the bad from being worse.'

Edeyn opened her mouth to make some other calf-brained

protest, and Giles, needing nothing from her now except to listen to Lady Lovell, cut in with, 'There's more fairness than it maybe seems. Martyn Gravesend was a bad-mouthed oaf who didn't know his place. Lionel has been too weak to be rid of him, so his demon did it for him. It's something Martyn has had coming to him for a long while, one way or another, and I'm not the only one who knows it.'

Edeyn turned toward him with a disbelief that might almost be rousing to actual anger – stupid woman – but he met her gaze and she had wit enough to read his expression rightly because she subsided. Lady Lovell, unnoticing, went on, 'We'll make it as right as we can. In all likelihood Giles will be given ward of the Knyvet lands. That would be the straightest way, since Giles is heir in fact. My lord will have say when it comes to it and will surely go that way. So your child's inheritance is safe. There's that to hold to.'

Edeyn, her head now bowed, moved a hand uncertainly, then laid it over her belly tentatively, protectively. Giles, taking advantage of the moment, went to her, knelt down, and laid his hand over hers as he said, 'Our son will make everything right. You see? In the long run of things it will all be well.'

Not lifting her head, Edeyn whispered, 'But not now. And never for Lionel.'

'For Lionel, too,' Giles said, tenderly because this was going exactly as he wanted it to. 'As well as we can make it. He'll have to be kept somewhere, guarded, because he can't be left loose anymore.'

Edeyn trembled, making a better fight against tears than he had thought was in her, but insisted, 'It isn't right. He isn't dangerous.'

God, but she could be ignorant! Forcing himself to go on with the tenderness, Giles said, 'But he is dangerous. Go see Martyn's body if you can't believe it otherwise.' She sobbed outright at that, her resistance finally breaking down, and he pressed on,

'Dear heart, we protected him for as long as we could. Now the only thing left is to ask for me to be given keeping of him as well as of his lands. That will be best all around. He'll still be confined, he has to be confined, but we'll see to him better than anyone else would, more kindly than anyone else would.'

Edeyn raised her head, looked to Lady Lovell with the beginning of hope. 'Would that be possible? Would that be allowed?'

'Very likely,' Lady Lovell said. 'I'll urge my lord to it, surely.'

Giles bowed his head to her in token of gratitude for the favour and kept a smile from his face while he did. They were making it all so beautifully easy for him, the fools. Even the few lies he had had to tell were so safe he hardly had to think twice about them. Martyn's death was so obviously Lionel's doing that even if Lord Lovell had been here, there would have been little trouble to it; and since as it stood he had only women to deal with, there was virtually no trouble at all except the necessity to bring the last pieces fully around his way. Let Edeyn finish with her stupid misery and weeping and there would be no more trouble in the matter except for what the law would make in the next few days, and then they could go home, with everything finally his, all his to manage as he wanted. Including Lionel.

Satisfied with Edeyn's help, unwitting though it had been, he gave her hand and belly a brisk pat and rose to his feet, taking her hands to draw her up to him. His arm around her waist, he said, 'You should come rest a while, dear heart. Lie down a little. For your sake and the child's.' He could leave her there to her maidservant and she could weep herself dry and be done with it.

But even as she gave way to him, leaned against him in that soft way he found best about her, she was protesting, 'Someone should go see how Lionel does. He's surely hurting. I could—'

'You could not!' Giles said, more harshly than he meant to but, God damn her, when was she going to grasp that Lionel was a murderer, unsafe, best left to rot wherever he had been put?

The tight circle of his arm kept Edeyn where she was as she

stiffened in an attempt to pull away, and before he had to make his hold more tight than that, the taller of the two nuns said, 'If you like, I can go to him, see how he does, and tell you of him.'

Edeyn gave way in Giles's hold, saying gratefully, 'Would you? That would be so good of you. You'll do it now?'

The nun bowed her head in an agreeing nod. Over Edeyn's head Giles thanked her, too. Gore-driven curiosity and the chance to talk about it afterwards were probably her real reasons for the offer, but she was welcome to indulge herself so far as he was concerned, so long as she served to keep Edeyn quiet. Gently again, because he had his way, he urged Edeyn toward the door, saying for everyone else's benefit, 'Now come, love. It's going to be well. I promise you. Come.'

Edeyn finally, even quietly, let him lead her out.

Chapter 13

FREVISSE COULD NOT recall the last time she had strongly had urge to slap someone's arrogant face, but Giles's barely concealed, contemptuous belief that he had to make things simple and plain for the poor women to understand him made her arm ache to do it. Was Edyn really so great a fool that she could tolerate him? Or did the unalterable fact of marriage force her to a self-preserving blindness?

Or was the fault in Frevisse herself, that she found Giles's insolence so intolerable?

She had, she knew, a low tolerance of fools. 'Judge not, that you be not judged' was a behest she had too often failed to follow. Through penance she had lessened the problem over the years but had lost much of her gain since Domina Alys had become prioress. And now she was falling into it yet again, judging Giles for his shallow sympathy at his cousin's plight and his unfeeling for Martyn's death which were simply a part of him, like the colour of hair or the set of eyes – something he could not help and something on which she should not judge him.

But he nonetheless scraped on her like a nail across stone and it was a relief to have him gone.

She curtsied to Lady Lovell and said, 'By your leave, I'll do as I promised Mistress Knyvet now.'

Lady Lovell nodded agreement with only partial attention.

Worry was drawn in around her eyes, her face tightened with unhappy thought. 'He's right about Lionel,' she said. 'He can never be free again. And yet most of the time he'll be utterly sane and aware of what's happened to him, of what he's done.'

'And of what he may do again,' Dame Claire said. 'A constant fear worse than the one he's already carried.'

Frevisse's gaze slid aside to the nearest window. Beyond it the garden lay bright in the early sunlight, the glint of dew still on the grass. Lady Lovell's women in their gay-coloured gowns stood or walked in little talking groups. Their mistress must have sent them there to be out of the way, and though there was no doubt at all that they were talking about Martyn's death, from here they were simply a loveliness in the lovely garden, far apart from the darkness of heart that she foresaw would be Lionel's life from now on.

'What is the broadest water and yet the safest to cross?' she heard herself saying.

Lady Lovell and Dame Claire both looked at her, puzzled. Frevisse shook her head, annoyed at herself; she had not meant to say it aloud. 'It's a riddle. Looking at the garden made me think of it. That's all.'

Dame Claire, willing to try to follow the way her mind was moving, said, 'It's not the water of death, is it? That's broad as eternity but hardly safe.'

'No. It's only dew on the grass. I'm sorry. I was remembering the riddle game Lionel, Edeyn, and Martyn shared, the delight they had in it, and I realized....'

She let the words trail off, not willing to finish the thought aloud. Lady Lovell did it for her, saying softly, sadly, '—That there won't be any more riddles now. Except the riddle of how to live with the knowledge of what he did.'

Frevisse nodded, crossed herself, curtsied, and left them.

As she reached the door into the great hall, she realized that she had neglected to ask where Lionel was imprisoned, but by the crowding of people and rabble of voices in the hall she doubted she would have trouble learning it from anyone she happened to ask. Probably no one in the entire manor was by now unaware of what had happened and most of them seemed to be here in the hall talking excitedly about it.

She backed away. In the nunnery she lived always in company, rarely alone, but it was a contained companionship, limited in numbers and noise, not this excess of both. She found she had no desire to walk into all of that. Besides, there was something else she should do before she went to Lionel, and she could learn where he was at the same time. With a small smile at her own mixed motive, she turned back to the stairs.

The chapel's antechamber was empty and quiet except for the low sound of men's voices in the chapel itself. When she went that way, a servant stepped out to turn her back, but before he said anything, she said, 'I've need to see Master Holt. Or Sire Benedict.'

The man accepted that, went back into the chapel, and a moment later reappeared to bid her enter. He looked as if he doubted the wisdom of it and also as if he were covertly interested in how she would react to what she saw. He obviously did not know she had been there already that morning, so that so far as she was concerned, there was nothing in particular to see. Martyn's body was gone and there were only the bloody places darkening the floor.

Master Holt stood over them with four other men including, Frevisse saw with surprise, young John Naylor. They looked up at her as she came to join them. Master Holt looked far more tired than any man should so early in a day, and grim, not particularly comforted by the fact that, 'At least the blood didn't go through into the parlour.' His look at her sharpened. 'Or did it? Is that what you've come about?'

'No. There's no blood below.' She was studying the stains. A large one, with part of an outline of one side of Lionel's body, marking where she remembered he had lain and where Martyn must have fallen across him. A lesser stain where the last blood had drained after Martyn had been thrown – or rolled or been pushed or however it had been – aside. And a third stain, much less that the other two....

Frevisse leaned toward it. The others were puddle thick, their edges definite. This one was more of a smear, well aside from the others and between where the bodies had been when she first saw them. She could not think, remembering the way Martyn and Lionel had lain then, how that one had been made.

She would have looked more but Master Holt was saying, 'That's good then. Though I'm not sure we'll ever have the stains fully out of the wood here. But we've seen enough.' He glanced at the other men for confirmation and they nodded agreement. 'So it can be cleaned now.'

Remembering why she had come, Frevisse said, 'Lady Lovell has asked me to see how Master Knyvet does, so his people can be told. Before I went to him I thought I'd learn what's been done with his man's body so I could tell him. He might have some comfort out of knowing.'

'God help him to any comfort he can find,' Master Holt said, meaning it, and Frevisse warmed toward him. 'The priests have taken the body to St Kenelm's, to see it cleansed and ready. Then it can be kept there for the crowner.'

So Martyn had been taken from the now un-hallowed chapel to the nearest sanctified place there was. That was kindness to a soul and body so abruptly parted, and more especially because, as Lionel had said yesterday, St Kenelm's life had likewise ended violently and too soon, had not been fully lived. He would make a good protector for a murdered man's soul.

It was an edged comfort to take to Lionel but better than none at all. 'And Master Knyvet?' she asked. 'Where is he being kept?'

'In the muniment room. It's the most secure place, with a lock and easily guarded,' Master Hold said. 'It's through the solar, off the other stairs. Deryk is on watch there. Tell him I said you could go in.'

Frevisse remembered the door from when she had come up the other way from the hall. She supposed this Deryk would take her word and thanked Master Holt, left the chapel, and crossed the antechamber to the solar.

Not everyone was in the great hall, it seemed. A clot of the ladies' chamber servants were gathered in the centre of the solar, talking eagerly. As Frevisse entered, they looked toward her, hopeful she would tell them more. Her hands tucked into her sleeves, she lowered her eyes and would have passed them by in contained silence but one of them dared to ask, 'You were in there, weren't you? In the chapel? Is it as terrible as they say?'

'I don't know what they say,' Frevisse answered without looking up or pausing.

'That there's blood everywhere, even on the altar, all over everything. That the bishop will have to come to send the demons away. That—'

Frevisse did not slow down but answered, 'There's blood on the floor where the men fell. That's all the blood there is. The altar is untouched.'

A woman stepped directly into her way, insisting, 'But is it true that—'

Frevisse stopped to stare directly into the woman's face, cutting her to silence, then saying, eyes cold and voice sharp-edged, 'Master Knyvet, when his demon seized on him last night, killed his steward there in the chapel. It's a grief to anyone who knows them. That's all you need to know about it and all anyone needs to say.'

Not that 'need' had aught to do with it. She had told them far less than they wanted to know, and they would say much more when she was gone, greedily feeding on other people's lives to put more feeling in their own. She had no help for that. She simply wanted to be away from them, and when she started forward, the woman moved aside hurriedly, leaving the way clear and asking no more questions of her as she crossed to the stairs and down the few steps to what had to be the muniment room.

A man undoubtedly Deryk stood purposefully in front of its closed, locked door. Broadly, stolidly built, his arms folded across the breast of his thick-woven brown doublet, his face set into a heavy-browed frown, he made an apparently formidable barrier against anyone going through the doorway; but at Frevisse's word that Master Holt had given leave for her to see the prisoner, his face unfurrowed into a mild grin. Without any question, he stepped aside to turn the key already set into the lock but, 'Mind the bitch,' he warned, the words rumbling good-naturedly in his chest. 'She growls if I try to move her, but likely you can step over her and she'll pay you no never mind.'

Frevisse glanced down in surprise to find Fidelitas at her feet, nose pressed to the crack below the door.

'Fidelitas,' Frevisse said and, when there was no response, bent down to stroke her head. She had forgotten all about her after Edeyn had set her down in the parlour. She must have slipped out and come here. 'Fidelitas, what is it, girl?'

The dog twitched a little under her hand but did not shift her concentration. What she wanted was on the other side of the door. Frevisse straightened and stepped back, still watching her, but Fidelitas gave her no notice, not even the flick of an ear. But when Deryk started to open the door, she came to her feet in a single leap, her tail and hindquarters frantic with approval, her nose now to the door's opening side.

'Here now,' Deryk said and would have reached for her, but Frevisse put out a staying hand.

'Let her go if it matters that much to her.'

Deryk hesitated, then shrugged and let Fidelitas push on in. But before he opened the door further, he dropped his voice to say, 'He's been quiet, but I'll leave the door wide while you're in so I can see and come put him down if he tries aught. You'll be safe enough, don't fear.'

It had not occurred to Frevisse to be afraid of Lionel, not with the fit over and surely no weapon left to hand, but she appreciated the thought and nodded her thanks as Deryk stepped out of her way and she went into the small, shadowed room.

This was where Lord Lovell kept much of his wealth and such record rolls as were most vital to him. It was built for security before all else, so the only window was a short, narrow slit in an outer wall. That and the open doorway behind her gave the only light to show the iron-bound chests ranged around the walls, heavily padlocked and chained to iron rings bolted into the walls. The room held nothing else except, now, Lionel, shackled at wrists and ankles and by a short run of chain to one of the iron rings in the wall.

He sat on one of the chests, bowed forward on himself as far as his hands would let him go, his head pressed between his hands. Neither the key nor the opening door had roused him, nor Frevisse's entrance, nor Fidelitas standing on her hind feet beside him, her forepaws on his leg, pawing at his knee to make him notice her.

Frevisse stopped where she was, not sure how near he would want her to come, not sure, now she came to think on it and saw how little he cared even that Fidelitas was there, that he would want her or anyone at all to see him.

But his want was not what had brought her here and her hesitation was barely momentary before she said, 'Master Knyvet.'

Lionel's head swung a little, side to side, showing he had heard her but refusing her more.

Refusing his refusal, she said, 'I've come to see how it is with you and to tell you what's been done with Martyn.'

The movement stopped. He waited and so did she until finally he straightened his body a little and raised his head toward her. No one had done anything to help him clean himself. His doublet all across one side was blackened and stiff with Martyn's dried blood, and the twist of his mouth showed that grief and horror were still fresh-gashed wounds in him. His unshaven face was sunken flesh over heavy bones as if grief had already eaten much of him away, and his voice was cracked with pleading as he said, 'Unless you've come to tell me that he isn't dead, that it's a mistake, that he's alive, only hurt, or that this is a nightmare that I'm in and you've come to wake me, there's no use in your being here.'

Frevisse had no good answer to that. The only ease for Lionel lay in lies she would not give him. He threw back his head, groaning with pain so inward it could have been his own death he felt, rather than Martyn's. Fidelitas pawed at him more desperately and tried to lick his face. Lionel wrenched his head sideways away from her and shoved her off him. 'No. I'm not worth anyone's care. Go away.' He struck, his hands a fist, at his bloodied clothing and cried at Frevisse, 'Look at me! It's true. Everything. All of it. Look! Oh, God.' He doubled over again, grasping his head between his hands, and began to rock forward and backward.

Frevisse went to him, took hold of his hands, forced him still, and said, 'Better you pray than this. Pray for him. Pray for you.' Because prayer would give him somewhere to go outside of his mind-wrenching grief, somewhere away from naked despair to a sort of hope, no matter how thin and useless hope must seem to him just now.

'Prayer,' Lionel groaned, denying it, not raising his head.

'Yes. Prayer.'

Lionel wrenched his head up and away from her. 'Prayer! Half my life I've prayed with everything that's in me and what's the answer I've been given? Death. Not even my own that I could be glad of! Not even that but Martyn's.' He groaned and curled more tightly in on himself. 'Martyn's death, not mine.' The pain burned from fire back to grey, aching despair again. In a bitter whisper he said, 'There's nothing in prayer.'

'There's your soul's salvation. *And Martyn's.*' She lashed the words at him, not for cruelty but because despair – wanhope – was among the great sins, and the last thing Lionel needed now was greater sin. Despair too long indulged in would become a form of madness more enduring than the one that had come on him last night. It would destroy him as utterly as Martyn had been destroyed, but in soul instead of body. If that happened, Martyn's death would have been merciful by comparison.

She hid her relief as Lionel flinched from what she said and then was still between her hands. She waited and in a while he said with something besides the blind pain that had driven him before, 'Martyn's soul?'

'He died in sin and suddenly,' Frevisse said, hardly less harshly than before, not letting her compassion show. 'His soul is surely in need of prayers.'

The horror he had awakened to this morning had wrenched Lionel out of a lifetime's belief. Now she was trying to wrench him back, and said a silent prayer of her own as a dull beginning of comprehension roused in his eyes. Slowly, he rubbed a hand across his face as if it ached; he probably did ache, in mind if not in flesh. Fidelitas was against his leg again, asking to be noticed, and his hand slid down to rest on the curve of her head. He drew a shallow, unsteady breath and asked, 'Where have they taken him?'

'To St Kenelm's, where you were yesterday.'

She said it gently. He had turned back at least a little from the blackness he had been going into, but it would take care to bring him the rest of the way. Why had Father Henry left him like this, alone to his despair? Sire Benedict had to come to him as soon as might be. All she could do was presently be glad that Lionel was nodding, accepting what she said, saying, 'Prayers. I can do that much. That least. I can pray for him.'

'And you'll be prayed for, too,' Frevisse said.

He shook his head, she did not know whether in refusal, or in dismissal of the idea as irrelevant to him now, or in disbelief that anyone would care. But he would pray and that would be well for his soul as well as Martyn's. That left his body still to be seen to.

'Have you been fed?'

Lionel shook his head, not caring.

Food then, and water for washing, and clean clothing. Each would be a step taking him further from last night. A step and then another step. A day and then another day. Frevisse had lived through regrets and griefs enough to know the healing help of time. Never a full cure, not for something that cut through to the soul like this, but healing enough that the hurt self could go on. Though what Lionel had to look forward to was maybe better not looked at too closely yet. Maybe for now it was enough that Fidelitas was leaned against his knee and his hand had begun, as if he were only distantly aware of it, to stroke her head. At least he had come that much back from the darkness. It was a small mercy, but just now any mercy was a welcome one.

Chapter 14

LEAVING DERYK WITH assurance that it was well for Fidelitas to stay with Lionel, Frevisse went on down the stairs to the great hall. The press of people was hardly less, but the talk had marginally diminished because someone had seen to having a table set up and breakfast finally laid out. Eating had perforce diminished talking.

From the advantage of the dais, Frevisse saw Dame Claire and Father Henry standing near the opposite door with bread and mugs of ale. Dame Claire was looking about her. Frevisse, when she saw she had been seen, raised a hand to her, both in greeting and in asking her to wait there. Dame Claire nodded agreement, and Frevisse went down among the folk around the table to find a share of food for herself. Way was made for her with respectful bobbing of the nearest heads, but she caught enough of the talk as she passed to tell it was still about Martyn's death and Lionel.

'It could have been anyone he killed,' a woman was declaring. 'The fit could have come on him anytime, anywhere, and he'd have been killing us with no warning at all. Why he's been left loose this long is what I'm wondering.'

'He'll be left loose no more, that's for sure,' a man answered her.

'A little late for that man of his,' someone returned.

'But not so late as it might be,' another woman declared. 'Now they'll lock him up and forget the key afterward sure.'

There was scant sympathy in anyone's tone; horror and indignation and gory-minded curiosity were all being indulged.

But Lionel and Martyn were *both* victims, Frevisse thought. Martyn was dead but Lionel had been used for his friend's death and then left to suffer for it.

Breakfast was ale and thick slices of bread with some of last night's beef on it. It was rich eating compared to nunnery fare, but Frevisse found that she was hungry enough not to care. A woman handed her a mug of ale as she reached for the bread and meat. Frevisse thanked her as she took it but found the kindness was not disinterested.

'You were there, weren't you?' the woman asked. She was wimpled and aproned in plain linen, one of the servants but too eager for talk to remember her place. 'In the chapel,' she urged, not relinquishing hold on the mug quite so quickly as she might have, to keep Frevisse's attention. 'You saw the body and all, didn't you?'

'Yes,' Frevisse answered with quelling lack of anything remotely like enthusiasm, but heads were turning, hoping for more from her, and she realized she might as well tell them. Lack of information would not stop their talk, and what they were not told, they would make up for themselves. Tersely she said, 'When I went in, they were lying on the floor, Master Knyvet unconscious, the way his demon always leaves him, Gravesend dead beside him. There was much blood—' They would want to hear that and it was the simple truth, but as she said it, she saw it again: the soaked darkness on and beyond Lionel's far side, the much lesser darkness spread down Martyn's throat and on the floor next to him. His bleeding must have been nearly done by the time he was thrown aside. And that lesser smear between them.

'Great gashing wounds they say they were,' one of the men put in, 'like he'd been slashed and slashed and slashed again.'

Frevisse shook her head, backing out from among them now

with her bread and ale, forgoing the cold meat. 'One wound. Just one.'

'I told you that,' said the woman who had handed her the ale, prodding the man in the ribs. 'His throat was slit, that was all. One stroke, neat as you'd please.'

Frevisse stopped her careful withdrawal from among them. Bread in one hand, ale in the other, she thought about what was wrong with what the woman had said.

No, not with what she had said, that had been right enough, but the wound....

More questions were being pressed at her. She shook her head at them and said, 'That's all there was. Nothing more. Just that,' and completed her escape, finally clear enough to circle around to Dame Claire and Father Henry.

They greeted her quietly, Dame Claire with, 'I would have warned you not to go among them. They're eager for anything anyone will say.'

'It was well enough. They want to know, that's all,' Frevisse said with somewhat less acidity than she would have a few moments ago. A single clean blow across the throat. She mentally shook herself – there were other things more immediately to hand – and said to Father Henry, 'Master Knyvet is in a bad way, in need of food and God's comfort. Is there aught else you should be doing or can you go to him now?'

The priest looked guiltily from his ale mug in one hand to the bread and meat in the other as if sorry to be caught with them. 'I can go now,' he said. 'I should have gone before. I'm sorry. There's been so much.'

He was shifting away from them even while he talked. Father Henry inspired her to annoyance more frequently than kindness, but his desire to do what ought to be done, if only he could think of it in time, was so complete, his earnestness so utterly unfeigned that sometimes, momentarily, like now, Frevisse regretted her impatience at him and suspected there might be

more virtue in his simplicity than she was capable of understanding. 'There's no need for over-haste, Father,' she said,
moderating her tone to reassure him. 'Finish your own breakfast
before you go.'

The priest nodded agreement but kept going, eating while he
went.

Dame Claire said, 'Eat. You look as if you need it.'

Frevisse looked at the food she held, remembered why she had
it, and began to eat, but while she did, she said, 'Lionel has
wakened into a nightmare he can't escape. It's probably the
worse because he has no memory of it.'

'If so, it's a nightmare of his own making,' Giles said behind
them.

They had been standing side by side, watching the folk in the
hall, their backs to the door that led to the chapel stairs. They
had not heard Giles approach, and Frevisse thought as she
looked at him startled over her left shoulder that he had not
meant they should. For preference she would have let him go
past them with no more acknowledgment than the inclination of
her head, but Dame Claire said, 'Of his own making?'

'You saw the liberties he let Gravesend take with him.
Gravesend acted more man to man than servant to master. He
was a bold one, a pushing one.'

'Master Knyvet seemed not to mind,' Dame Claire said.

'What could he do except tolerate him? He wasn't likely to
find many fools willing to see him through his fits. He'd put
himself at Gravesend's mercy and had no way out. Except the
one he took.'

Dame Claire made a small, protesting noise. Giles shrugged
and smiled a sad but accepting smile. 'Not on purpose, I'm sure.
But I can't help wonder if he didn't give himself a little more
willingly than usual to his demon's purpose this time. Even
Lionel's tolerance with Gravesend must have been worn thin in
places by now, provoked once too often by Gravesend's pushing.

Ah well.' He shrugged again, a deprecating gesture, suggesting they need not pay too much heed to his musings. 'We'll never know. It's a pity from beginning to end and that's the sum of it. But those of us that live still need to eat. Pray you, pardon me.'

He bowed, they inclined their heads to him, and he went on his way toward the breakfast table. They watched him go and when he was well away, Dame Claire said thoughtfully, 'Why don't I like him?'

'Because, among other things, what passes in a household should stay in a household, not be bandied about to people barely met and barely known,' Frevisse answered. He had no reason except nastiness to be saying so much to them about either Lionel or Martyn. The more especially because up to now he had shown no inclination at all for even their company, let alone their conversation. 'Here.' Frevisse put the ale mug and what was left of her bread into Dame Claire's hand. 'Wait for me.'

Dame Claire took them without question. She went through the world differently than Frevisse did, seeing matters in her own way, but they understood each other well enough, and in the nunnery had learned to use their different ways to the same ends more often than not. So she stayed where she was and did not question, and Frevisse, as if she had eaten all her food and wanted more, went back toward the breakfast table.

Making no haste about it, she eased in among the folk still there, not far aside from Giles but without seeming to heed him, all her apparent intention on more food. If anyone noticed she had been there before, she would present an unfortunate picture of gluttony; but she doubted anyone would bother with her at all, not with Giles there, willingly talking about what everyone wanted to hear. As she knifed a small piece of meat onto a slice of bread he was saying, 'Hai, Petir, feeling better about old Martyn now? He's done for you for the last time, hasn't he?'

The man he spoke to shied back a little with a twitch of a smile and uncertain shrug. He was somewhere in his middle years, sallow and thin-haired and bent about the shoulders. Frevisse remembered the dismissed servant John Naylor had mentioned and guessed this was he even before Giles said for everyone to hear, 'Gravesend had him sent off. Turned Lionel against him for no good reason except Martyn didn't like him. There's more people than my poor cousin with cause to hate old Gravesend. The only wonder is someone didn't see to him sooner.' He crossed himself. 'But it's still pity it came to this. Pity and shame to us all.' He crossed himself again. A few hands echoed the gesture and his head's sad shaking but it was not piety they wanted, it was talk. Giles clapped Petir on the shoulder and leaned closer to whisper something in his ear. Petir responded with what he tried to make a grin but he managed no more than a sickly twitch of his mouth. Giles clapped him again and went on his way down the hall.

The talk did not pick up behind him. He had not given much new fodder to keep it going. Then sight of Master Holt come into the hall's far end with John Naylor seemed to remind everyone it was past time they were about their morning duties. Suddenly everyone was scattering, looking very intent on work somewhere else, except a few who stayed to clear the table – and Petir, who set instead to refilling his ale mug. Frevisse went to stand beside him. He looked around at her and made a respectful bow.

'Ale, my lady?'

'No. But thanks.' She doubted she would have long to talk with him and said, hoping surprise would serve as well as acquaintance might have, 'What did Master Giles say to you just now?'

Startlement made Petir look slightly stupid for a moment. Then he gathered his wits and said, 'Naught fit for a lady to hear.'

'Was it about Gravesend's death?'

'It was that.'

'Then I'd like to hear it. I saw the body. There's little left to shock me with. And Lady Lovell wants to know what's being said.' That last was a pulling at the corners of truth, but Frevisse was beginning to think that if decisions were going to be made concerning what became of Lionel and his properties, Lady Lovell should know more than she apparently did so far about Giles.

Petir hesitated, but he was more used to giving way than going his own, and said down into his ale mug, 'He said that Gravesend had two mouths now but neither of them will be talking anymore.'

'You don't like Master Giles.'

It was not a fair question to ask a servant, but she wanted to see at least his reaction even if he did not answer. He said nothing but his eyes flicked up at her and away down the hall where Giles had gone, then back to the ale mug. Pushing a little farther, Frevisse tried, 'It's said it was Gravesend who had you dismissed from the Knyvet household. Did he?'

That much Petir would admit to. 'He did that, aye. Told me I'd do better elsewhere.'

'And you were angry at him.'

'Angry at him? Aye.' Petir's expression pulled toward a frown. 'Aye, I'm still angry. It wasn't me should have been sent away.' He quickly crossed himself. 'But he's a dead man now and I'll pray for him like I ought. It wasn't all his doing, but he shouldn't have done it anyway.'

Frevisse pressed gently, knowing how easily most people could be led on to talk about themselves. 'Not all his doing?' she asked.

'Nay, it was because of Master Giles. He's the one who didn't want me around and pushed it until Gravesend sent me off. I knew—'

He was warming under the chance to tell his grievance, but a man called, 'Petir!' from the hall's end and jerked a hand impatiently at him. Petir took a long pull from his mug, gave Frevisse a hasty bow, and begged her pardon, he had to go.

Quickly, before he could, Frevisse said, 'But you're doing well enough now, working here. How did that come about?'

'She saw to it. Mistress Edeyn. Didn't let them have it all their own way, she didn't.' He ran the words together in his haste, drawing away while he said them, but the warmth in them was far different from his heat against Martyn and Giles. As he hurried off, Frevisse wondered if Edeyn knew she had an admirer. And how much did that have to do with Giles and Martyn's desire to send him off? What else went on in that household she had no idea of?

At her shoulder Dame Claire said, 'We haven't done morning prayers yet and it must be nearing time for Sext. This is all none of your business, you know.'

'Lady Lovell needs to know what's being said, how things are running among her people,' Frevisse answered.

With unveiled amusement, Dame Claire promptly pointed out, 'She has people enough of her own to tell her that. You need better justification than that for your arrant curiosity.'

'I wanted to know if we were the only ones whom Master Giles is so favouring with confidences about family matters that are none of our business.'

'And we aren't.'

'Not by any means. In fact I'd guess we were a little slighted of the more amusing bits he has to offer.'

'The burden of being a nun. Who was that you were talking with just now?'

'A slighted servant with grievances against both Master Giles and Martyn and a warm admiration of Mistress Edeyn.'

With suddenly no amusement at all, Dame Claire asked, 'Are you finding complications where no one else is?'

'Not about the servant, no. That's something done with.

Unless you want to think he lay in wait and crept in last night and killed Martyn and made it look like Lionel did it.'

'I don't want to think that, no,' Dame Claire said. 'He looked more the sort who would be too worried to lie in wait, let alone actually go through with something that vile. And you don't think it of him either.'

'No, I don't. No, what I'm thinking is that the more I see and learn about Master Giles, the less I think it would be a good thing if he were given keeping of Lionel when all this is over.'

Dame Claire did not answer that, said instead, after a pause, 'And what are you thinking to do now?'

'What I said I would do. Go and tell Edeyn how it is with Lionel.'

Chapter 15

THE DOOR TO the Knyvets' chamber was shut. Frevisse tapped at it lightly, not wanting to rouse Edeyn if she had somehow been able to fall asleep, or even was only resting; but the maid-servant who jerked it open after hardly a pause was clearly not concerned with anyone's rest. She was flushed and purse-mouthed with anger or aggravation that she should have smoothed over before she opened the door. Now, confronted by two nuns, she dragged her face into a semblance of politeness, succeeding before she said, 'My ladies?'

Taller than the maidservant, Frevisse was able to see beyond her to a trunk standing open and a disarray of clothing around it. Her manners losing ground to curiosity, she moved forward, saying brightly, 'We've come to see Mistress Knyvet,' giving the maid no choice but to move back or be run into.

The woman deftly hopped backward while saying, 'Mistress Knyvet has gone out.'

That paused Frevisse. 'Gone out?'

The woman nodded and added helpfully, 'She isn't here.'

Frevisse was far enough into the room now to see that for herself. 'I have something to tell her. She was expecting me.'

'Oh, she'll be back directly. She's only gone to the church. To take the good shroud Lady Lovell gave her for Master Gravesend.' The maid's face fell. She seemed to go readily from one emotion to another, her face showing each one as it came.

'I'd have taken it, but she said she particularly wanted to, that he'd no family and Master Knyvet couldn't – well, I should hope not, wouldn't you? – and someone ought to see to him other than just a servant. So she's gone.'

'And those are Gravesend's things?' Frevisse asked, with a nod toward the disordered chest. Dame Claire, behind her and only a little through the doorway, prodded her in the back in reminder of how far she should not go.

Frevisse ignored her, watching the maid's face go back to the sour, angry look it had had when she opened the door. 'That lot? Not likely. Master Gravesend, he travels – travelled with a bag and a little box and is done with it. That's Master Giles's lot and a pretty mess he's made of it, too.'

'And left you to put it to rights,' Frevisse guessed sympathetically.

'You have the right of that.' The woman went off to pick up a shirt from the floor by one sleeve and shake it. 'Now that was pressed and folded and put away tidy as you could please. All of this was, and he'd no cause to go digging away for anything. He's but to ask to have it fetched to him. He's done that right enough all these years. Never turn a hand to it when there's someone else he can order, that's his way. He's been known to wait an hour rather than do a thing himself that would take a minute. So what am I to think when I open this chest a little ago and find it's been turned and tossed inside like this?'

'And you know it was Master Giles did it?' Frevisse asked. Dame Claire prodded her in the back again. 'It wasn't another of the servants?'

'Not likely,' the maid said. 'They're not so careless. And besides he was here when I opened it and when I cried out at it, he says, does Master Giles, laughing like he does when someone's been given a fret, "You've made a right mess of that, girl. It'd better be put to rights the next time I look in there." As if I'd made a mess like this! Oh, I've made the mess bigger,

163

spreading it out, but how else am I to fold and sort it all back to place again if I don't? But that's how I knew he'd done it himself because if he'd really thought it was me, I'd have felt his stick on me right enough. Well, his hand because he doesn't have his stick when he travels with Master Knyvet. Master Knyvet doesn't hold with it.' Tears filled her eyes as a new thought and turn of feeling took her. 'Isn't it pitiful about Master Knyvet? Mad, they say, and all his wits gone, just like that, and Master Gravesend dead because of it. I'd have taken that shroud for Mistress Edeyn. I liked Master Gravesend as well as anybody, he was that good-hearted a man and never a meanness to anyone.'

Her glare through her tears at the rumpled clothing told of another who was nothing like that, but before she said so, Frevisse said, 'Our thanks. We'll seek out Mistress Edeyn in the church then.'

The maid, sniffing on tears and indignation, saw them out and closed the door behind them, the offended shirt still in her hand.

'Well, you've taken to listening to tale-telling like I've never known you to do,' Dame Claire observed when they were alone.

'I certainly have.' Frevisse frowned over that truth, unable to deny it, unable to explain it, even to herself.

'Are you going to tell me why?' Dame Claire asked gently.

'I don't know yet. Except....' Her voice trailed off. She could not offer Dame Claire anything at all for explanation. She had none, only an unease.

'Except you need to,' Dame Claire said.

'Except I need to,' Frevisse agreed, trying to sort through her thoughts and, more tenuous but as real, her feelings.

'Are we going to Edeyn?'

Frevisse roused with a small shake of her head at herself and said, 'We'd best.'

The great hall was clear of everyone, and the garden when they came out into it was empty of people except for a gardener and his boy making their way along the beds in search of weeds.

Frevisse half-supposed they would meet Edeyn returning from the church since her errand was only a short one, but they did not and found her the next place Frevisse supposed she would be, kneeling before the altar almost where Lionel had been yesterday.

There was no shroud nor was Martyn's body present, and quite deliberately Frevisse led Dame Claire up the short nave to near where Edeyn was, to make her aware that they were there. As they stopped a few yards aside from her, to kneel briefly to their own prayers, Edeyn looked sideways at them, and when they stood up she rose with them.

'Lionel?' she asked.

'Fidelitas is with him. She seems to be helping.' It was the only comforting thing that came to Frevisse's mind so she said it first. 'But he's hurting. Not in body,' she added quickly at Edeyn's immediate, sharp alarm. 'In mind. For what he's done. For Martyn.'

'But he remembers nothing of it, does he?' Edeyn asked softly.

'Nothing at all. I think that adds to the pain. To have not even known he had done it, the mindlessness was so complete.'

'He's always hated that he knows nothing while an attack is on him,' Edeyn said.

'Where's Master Gravesend?' Dame Claire asked.

Edeyn nodded toward a side door. 'They have him in the sacristy until he's cleansed and shrouded, to not risk blood in here, too.'

Because there was no way to ask reasonable permission to do what she wanted to do, Frevisse neither asked nor said anything but went to the sacristy door, knocked once, and entered. Behind her Dame Claire made what might have been the beginning of a protest but it was too late to be of use. Inside, Sire Benedict and the two servants he was overseeing at their work looked up in surprise from Martyn's stripped body.

'Good my lady!' the priest began in startled protest, and stepped between her and Martyn's body.

As if anything could be more indecent than the wound that had killed him, Frevisse thought, and that she had long since seen more than clearly enough. Besides, it was not Martyn's body for which she was there. His soiled clothing was dumped in a heap on the floor near the door, and for something like courtesy's sake she said, 'Good Father,' in greeting to Sire Benedict but stopped even as she did, to pick up first one and then the other of Martyn's shoes, look at their soles, and drop them again, all so quickly that the priest was still gathering himself to say something else to her as she straightened, gave him a slight curtsy, and withdrew, shutting the door as she went.

Edeyn, too wrapped in her own feelings to be curious over it, paid no heed to her return but went on telling Dame Claire, 'He'll likely be buried here. He has no family living, and Giles says the trouble of taking him back to Knyvet when there's no one of his own folk there isn't worth it.'

Giles would say that, not bothering to consider what Lionel's wish in the matter might be, Frevisse thought tartly. For Giles, Lionel was already only baggage to be dealt with, no longer a person. But she kept the thought to herself. Almost the only improvement she had noticed in herself was an occasional tendency toward discretion, probably come with age.

'I'll see to masses being said,' Edeyn was going on. They had begun to walk down the nave together, Edeyn between the nuns and talking as if words were a shield against too many thoughts. 'Beginning as soon as may be. He can't be buried until the crowner has come but the masses can be started. Will I be able to see Lionel soon?'

That last came as they reached the door that stood open into the porch. Frevisse answered as straightly as she could, 'I don't know. Not for a while, I'd think.'

'But he's being seen to, isn't he? He's as well as may be?'

'For now. I hope it can be made better when we understand a little more.'

'What more is there to understand?' Giles asked, appearing at the porch's outer end, dark against the sunlight. 'My cousin in his madness murdered someone and because we can never know when that madness will come on him again, there's nothing for it but to keep him locked away the rest of his days.'

'I thought there were signs when an attack was about to come,' Dame Claire said. 'Warnings.'

Frevisse would have said it first, but her sudden anger at Giles for being so suddenly there and so plainly having overheard them made her hold her tongue until she was sure of what would come off it.

'Yes,' Edeyn said readily. 'There's one. He feels it in his flesh, in his left hand, an oddness that warns him when one is near.'

'It's his demon crawling back inside him,' Giles said, 'and now that we know what comes of it, who's likely to want to be near him when it happens after this? Martyn was fool enough to do it and look where he is.'

What he said was probably true enough, but he could have said it with less satisfaction, Frevisse thought and still held her tongue, leaving it to Dame Claire to say, 'Yes, well, I daresay you have the right of it. My lady, if you'll excuse us, we should be going.'

She was drawing away while she spoke, and though it seemed less than kind to leave Edeyn to her husband's untenderness, Frevisse could think of no excuse to linger and she went with Dame Claire, the both of them circling Giles when he did not bother to stand aside to let them pass.

Chapter 16

LUCE MET THEM in the garden with word that Lady Lovell wished to see them. She was subdued, without her usual chatter, while she led them not to the parlour but the room where they had dealt with Lady Lovell over the nunnery business yesterday. She announced them at the door but left them to go in to Lady Lovell alone.

She was at the table as she had been yesterday. Her son Harry was not with her, but the clerks were at their tables, working in the warm sunlight through the southward window with its view of the purposeful come and go of people across the yard. From the west wing came the clear sounds of the stonemasons at their building: the chink of metal on stone, the creak of the lift-wheel, occasional good-humoured shouts and orders. By every outward sign Minster Lovell was well along in a day as pleasant and well ordered as yesterday had been.

But outwardly was not all there was to anything. As they had passed the stairs on the way to here, Frevisse had been sharply conscious of Lionel in his small prison above them, so near to everything, able to hear so much of it, and yet so hopelessly cut off from the day and everything there should have been for him. Almost, in his way, as cut off from it as Martyn was, but without the accompanying grace of oblivion.

Frevisse wondered how much of that thought was with Lady Lovell, too, because though she stood where she had yesterday, with her work spread out in front of her and a smile of greeting for them, her lightness and laughter were gone behind a dark sadness in her eyes, though she inclined her head to their low curtsies and said warmly, 'My ladies. We're trying to put the day back somewhere near to where it should be and go on with what needs doing. I talked with Master Holt and with your John Naylor yesterday, as you suggested, and have thought on the matter since. You may like what I've bethought me of.'

'At your pleasure, my lady,' Dame Claire said.

'It would seem from your customal that it was indeed by the Lovell responsibility the well was last made, with the nunnery to have the main share thereafter in its upkeep. We all agree the nunnery has done its share heretofore, but the wear of time goes on and the well now needs to be deepened and the stonework remade anew. Agreed?'

Dame Claire and Frevisse indicated that was exactly the case. It had taken Domina Alys far more words and a great deal more temper to say the same.

'The argument lies in who is to bear the cost of this new work, my steward claiming it should be the nunnery as part of the upkeep, the nunnery claiming it is ours because the well must virtually be made new and that is Lord Lovell's duty.'

'Yes, my lady,' Dame Claire said. Frevisse made a small nod of agreement. That was exactly it.

'To my mind,' Lady Lovell said, 'your customal is not precise on the matter. It states what was done then without clearly saying what should follow afterward in the fullness of time.'

'We tend to forget the fullness of time,' Frevisse said, 'if the need of the moment has been satisfied.'

'Too often too true.' Lady Lovell smiled. 'That seems to be what happened here, certainly. There's wide possibility for argument, with nothing to bring the matter clearly down on one side or the other. So what I've to suggest – and Master Holt and your John Naylor both thought satisfactory to both sides – is that Lord

Lovell undertake to find a master mason to oversee the work, so it should be well and expertly done, and pay him and for a work-ale afterward when the well is finished, while the nunnery would provide the men and the stone for the work itself. What think you? Would that satisfy?'

Dame Claire and Frevisse looked at each other. It was not precisely what Domina Alys wanted. Her desire was for everything to be at Lord Lovell's cost and Lord Lovell's effort, but this might be something she would accept because priory men could be set to the task at no cost in silver to the priory and there was stone enough about that there would be no need to spend anything on that either except the men's time to gather it. 'I think,' Dame Claire said slowly, 'that we could take that offer to our prioress in good faith and reasonable hope.'

'I'll have a letter made to my steward there and another to your prioress for you to take when you leave.'

Lady Lovell appeared as pleased as Frevisse would have been if she had been unaware of Domina Alys's ability to refuse even so fair an offer. But sufficient to the day were the troubles thereof and she smiled with Lady Lovell and Dame Claire who said, 'Our thanks, my lady. We can go whenever the letters are ready. This afternoon if you wish.'

One of the benefits of travelling with virtually nothing was that it took virtually no time to be on their way, but Lady Lovell said, still smiling, 'Then I shall see they are not written until later, so that you can stay another night at least. Unless there's need for haste?'

'No need at all,' Dame Claire answered.

That was true and to Frevisse's mind leaving in the morning would be far better. It would do Dame Claire no harm to have another day to rest, and if they left in the morning rather than the afternoon, they should reach Oxford and its priory by tomorrow night instead of spending another night on the road. And it would give her the remainder of the day to ask for answers to questions she would not like to leave unfinished behind her.

She had been refusing to admit to herself how increasingly uneasy she was over Martyn's death until it had momentarily seemed she would have to leave it behind her. Her rush of relief at not having to leave yet told her how important her questions were becoming to her, how deep her unease was running. Deep enough that although Dame Claire was finishing their thanks and beginning to withdraw, to leave Lady Lovell to all her other business, Frevisse asked, 'Has anything further been decided about Master Knyvet?'

Dame Claire cast Frevisse a glance of annoyance, and the satisfaction in a problem well handled went out of Lady Lovell's face as the greater problem that could not be so easily seen to came back to her. 'Nothing can really be done or decided now until the crowner comes. He's been sent for but how long until he's here depends on when and where he's found and if he's free to come immediately.'

'Until he comes—' Frevisse began hesitantly.

'Dame Frevisse!' Dame Claire said quellingly.

Frevisse with an effort stopped herself from going on, but Lady Lovell looked from one to the other and said, 'Yes?'

Frevisse looked toward the clerks at their work, too near across the room. Lady Lovell understood and moved away, toward the room's far end, drawing Frevisse and Dame Claire after her. When they were as away from the clerks as the room would allow, she said again, 'Yes?'

Avoiding Dame Claire's displeased look, Frevisse said, 'There are things I'm not sure of about Martyn's death.'

Dame Claire made an exasperated sound.

Levelly Lady Lovell asked, 'Such as?'

Frevisse gathered her inarticulated unease into words, to make it clear to herself for the first time, as well as to Lady Lovell. 'The way they were lying – Lionel and Martyn – it doesn't agree with where the blood was.'

'Where the blood was?' Lady Lovell asked, not understanding, asking Frevisse to make it clearer.

'Martyn's blood is on Lionel's clothing in a way that makes it seem Martyn must have fallen across him and bled there before being pushed aside to lie where he was found, beside Lionel.'

'The blood might have sprayed when the wound was made,' Lady Lovell suggested. 'Before Martyn fell. It will when a throat is cut.'

'Only when it's cut low. Martyn's wound was high under the throat. Blood doesn't spray from a wound that high.' It had been years since she had ridden to a hunt, in her girlhood before she entered St Frideswide's, but she remembered that much about kills.

Lady Lovell nodded agreement. Hunting was still part of her life and she had seen deaths enough to understand the difference.

'And the blood was all in one place,' Frevisse said. 'On Lionel's side and the floor beside him, as if drained, not spattered.' The more she said, the more wrong everything she had seen in the chapel became. So long as she had not thought in detail about it, it had been simply enough, but now…. In fairness she tried to make what it had seemed at first be possible. 'It might be that Lionel fell even as he struck the blow and Martyn fell dying onto him. But then how did Martyn end up stretched out beside him instead of across him?'

'A last death spasm?' Lady Lovell offered. 'Or by Lionel's movement? It's said he flings about wildly when the fit is on him.'

'But he was lying stretched out on his back as if to rest, as if he had been carefully placed that way. And the blood on the floor wasn't smeared, as it should have been if he had moved that violently. It looked as if he fell and Martyn fell across him, bleeding, and then Lionel never moved at all but Martyn did.'

'Then it had to be a last spasm by Martyn?' Lady Lovell asked, not refusing the problem Frevisse was making but considering other possibilities.

Frevisse held silent. It would be so simple if that were it. But … 'I don't know.' She turned to Dame Claire. 'How much would a man likely move after a wound like that? After bleeding as much as he did over Lionel?'

Unwillingly, Dame Claire said slowly, 'It was a very great deal of blood. Martyn was assuredly unconscious and probably fully dead as he lay on Lionel, there was so much blood there. He might … twitch. The body sometimes does when death comes too suddenly. But to move enough to be—' Dame Claire stopped, apparently trying to remember in greater detail than she had wanted to what she had seen in the chapel. Even more slowly than before, she finished, '—to be lying as far away from Lionel as he was, no, I don't see how he could.'

Though she had found her way through the words almost one by one, not liking them even as she said them, she was sure of what she said. The three women looked at one another. If it could not have been what it had so readily seemed, what *had* happened?

Carefully Frevisse said, 'There was a thin smear of what I thought was blood on the bare floor between the bodies. As if from a' – it was harder to say it than it had been to think it – 'a foot.'

'A footprint?' Dame Claire asked.

'No. Nothing so definite. A smear. Not even foot-sized.'

'There was so much blood,' Lady Lovell offered. 'This was simply more.'

'All the rest of the blood there was thick, had flowed over Lionel, over Martyn. This was apart from both of them and smeared thin.'

Dame Claire began to make what looked to be an objection but stopped and waited, her gaze going from Frevisse's face to Lady Lovell's and back again. Lady Lovell said nothing at all for a long moment, then, lifted her skirt a little, put out her slippered foot, and slid it slightly across the floor. 'Smeared like that?'

Frevisse nodded. 'Like that. As if there had been blood on just the forepart of a shoe and the foot had slipped and smeared it.'

'Neither of them could have stepped in the blood after the blow was struck?' Lady Lovell asked.

'I've already looked at Martyn's shoes and there was nothing. I want to look at Lionel's.'

'It might have been Sire Benedict or your priest, careless when they first came in and found them.'

'The smear was dark and dried. It had been there longer than that.'

'Long enough that maybe someone came in well before then, came close enough to step in the blood, and left without raising a cry for some reason or other?'

'They might have,' Frevisse conceded.

'Or it wasn't blood at all but a stain already on the chapel floor,' Dame Claire suggested.

'Then it will still be there when I go back to look again,' Frevisse said.

'The chapel is new,' Lady Lovell said. 'There had better be no stains on its floor.'

'The wound,' Dame Claire said as if startled.

Frevisse and Lady Lovell looked at her. 'The wound?' Frevisse asked.

'The wound!' Dame Claire gestured toward her throat, trying to make them see. 'It was a single slash across his throat. A single, clean wound. Only that one. Do you see?'

Belatedly, Frevisse did, finally able to grasp what had made her uneasy when she had spoken of Martyn's death to the servants. And judging by Lady Lovell's soft exclamation, she saw it, too. Despite all the talk of Lionel killing in a demon-driven frenzy, there was only the one wound. No wild slashing or stabbing or signs of struggle. One wound and....

Lady Lovell completed Frevisse's thought aloud, 'And it had to have been made from behind, to have been put like that across his throat so cleanly and high up.' The way the huntsman finished a deer in the hunting field, by straddling its downed body, jerking back the head, and slicing open the throat, not from in front but from behind.

They looked at each other, all with the same question, but it was Lady Lovell who finally said it aloud.

'What was Martyn doing with his back to Lionel?'

Chapter 17

NEITHER FREVISSE NOR Dame Claire made answer to that. For Martyn to turn his back on Lionel, to be so distracted as to let his dagger be taken and his throat be cut by the man he was there to watch and help....

'And then for Lionel to fall and be lying perfectly straight on his back with his hands arranged on his breast, and Martyn to wait until then before falling across him,' Frevisse said slowly. 'That doesn't make sense.'

Lady Lovell, her voice as even and almost as pleasant as usual but with a hard anger in her eyes, said, 'Apparently there's going to be more for the crowner to ask about than we thought at first. Dame Claire, will you do something more than you have already?'

Somewhat unwillingly, Dame Claire nodded.

'Would you see if Sire Benedict or your priest have blood on their shoe soles? I can't think of any way to find out except by asking to see them, but if you could do it so they don't know that it matters, it would be better. Can you do that?'

'Yes, my lady. Father Henry has only the one pair of shoes, I know, but does Sire Benedict have more so he could have changed?'

'He has only the one pair and they're new ones, part of his Easter livery. He always gives his old ones away afterward, for charity's sake and to have no more than he needs. Dame

Frevisse, as well as Lionel's shoes, would you find out exactly what happens in his attacks? I've always let it be enough for me to know he has them and to pray for him and made a point not to pry beyond that. Enough people pry at him, he's needed a few friends who don't. But maybe if we know more about them, we'll find we've only misunderstood something and there's no problem after all.'

Unhesitatingly Frevisse said, 'Yes, my lady,' ignoring Dame Claire's sideways look at her that said she suspected Frevisse would have tried anyway, asked or not.

Lady Lovell shook her head. 'I don't want to be doubting where there was no doubt, but if it's possible Martyn didn't die the way we thought, if it's possible Lionel didn't kill him, then—' She stopped but what she did not say was there in the silence with them.

If Lionel had not killed Martyn, then someone else had, and while Lionel was chained with his despair in the dark room, the murderer was still free among them.

In the great hall after they had left Lady Lovell, Dame Claire said, 'Before anything, I think we should go to the chapel for at least one of the morning's offices. We've done none of them.'

With sharp guilt, Frevisse realized that was true. Yesterday she had been missing St Frideswide's familiar ways; today she had forgone everything that made St Frideswide's most precious to her. She bent her head in quick agreement. 'In the chapel?'

It had been blood-polluted, but it was quiet and apart from the general bustle of the household, still a good place to pray.

Dame Claire agreed with a nod, adding, 'Besides, I doubt I could draw you as far away as the church again, could I? Not with your mind all turned to this.'

Frevisse knew how little Dame Claire had liked her morning spent in what had seemed indulgent curiosity and too much talk. 'Dame Claire, I'm sorry.'

'Sorry for asking questions? You always ask questions. And it seems this time you're in the right with them. There seem to be questions that ought to be asked before Lionel is condemned. But there are also prayers to be said.'

She said it without irk or anger, only firmly, and did not wait for more agreement but led the way back to the stairs that would take them up to the solar rather than across the hall now busy with servants beginning to set up the tables for dinner. Frevisse followed, meaning to say nothing else, but as they came to Lionel's guarded door, with Deryk still outside it, she said, 'Wait only a moment, I pray you.' Before Dame Claire had turned around to ask her why, she said, 'Deryk, I need to see Master Knyvet again.'

Behind her, Dame Claire made a disapproving noise, but Deryk was already unlocking the door without question or hesitation, and when he opened it and stood aside, Frevisse went in without looking back to see how annoyed Dame Claire now was.

The thin band of sunlight through the slit window had strengthened since early morning, but even so the room would have been mostly darkness until the door opened, letting in the fuller light from the stairs. Lionel, still seated where she had left him, slumped forward on the chest, did not respond. Only Fidelitas, still leaning against his knee, lifted her head to see who had come. To one side the food Father Henry must have brought him sat on the floor untouched even by Fidelitas.

There was no particular point in talk. What comfort she could offer, she had offered before, so she simply said, 'Let me see the bottom of your shoes.'

Lionel stirred and looked at her, not speaking but visibly working to draw his mind back from whatever darkness it had reached. Finally, more slowly than Frevisse's impatience would have liked, he grasped what she had asked of him and lifted his left foot and cocked his knee to bend his foot toward the doorway and the light. There was nothing on the sole beyond expected scuffs.

'Your other one,' she said.

There was no blood on it either, but this time as he set it down he asked, 'Why?'

She could not tell him, not with Deryk there to hear and the chance it would not come to anything after all. 'There are people who care about you. Hold to that. Remember it.'

Fidelitas whined small in her throat and nudged her muzzle against his arm. Lionel moved his free hand to the nape of her neck and sank his fingers into her fur, holding to it as if to a lifeline.

Frevisse drew back and let Deryk close the door.

'Has anyone besides Father Henry come to him?' she asked.

'Only our priest, and he didn't do good with him either,' Deryk readily answered.

Dame Claire said nothing to her at all, simply turned away and went on to the chapel. It smelled of lye and scrubbing and had a barren air, with the long woven carpet rolled up from across the floor to lie in front of the altar that now was stripped of its white covering and all the things that had stood on it. Over it the lamp hung dark.

But the chapel was still a good place for prayer, a place where holiness had been, and quiet and apart from the household bustle. Frevisse and Dame Claire went past the large damp places where the scrubbing had been done to kneel in front of the altar. Times for the early and mid-morning Offices were long past, but it was close to the time for Nones and they settled to the prayers and psalms together. Frevisse knew she took too long to draw her mind fully into them but thought she had managed it until at the end, while she was saying, correctly, with Dame Claire, the Paschaltide responsory of *Alleluia, alleluia, alleluia*, she found she was thinking, far more strongly, the prayer from the end of None. *Misericordia et veritas praecedent faciem tuam, Domine.* Mercy and truth go before you, Lord.

In the head-bowed silence after they had finished, she went on praying for that. For mercy and truth. And that there would be mercy in the truth once it was found.

If it was found.

Chapter 18

IT WAS TIME for dinner when they finished, and though Frevisse dreaded the talk there would be with so many people brought together for the first time since this morning, there was no choice but to go.

It helped that she and Dame Claire were at the high table, though their company there was noticeably diminished not only by Lionel's absence but by that of Giles and Edeyn and Sire Benedict. Lady Lovell saw to it that the talk around her was kept to ordinary things, but enough snatches and scraps of conversation from the lower tables reached Frevisse to make plain there was no restraint there. It seemed interest in the general bloodiness of the murder had eased in favour of speculation over Lionel. It did not matter that it was understood he had only killed because he was possessed. That warranted pity and pity was granted, in limited amounts; but it warranted fear, too, because what could be expected of a man so readily seized on, so readily driven out of his mind? And with the fear went indignation that – like the fear – was the more enjoyable because it could both be safely indulged in and was so undeniably justified.

With dinner over and the household scattering to their afternoon tasks, Dame Claire said, 'I'll speak to Father Henry before he goes and find Sire Benedict afterward. What are you about?'

'I want to talk to Edeyn about Lionel's fits.'

Dame Claire went away toward Father Henry where he was in

talk with some officer of the household about coursing hares, to judge by their gestures.

Frevisse made her own way through the thinning shift of people, picking up snippets of talk as she went, most of it no different from the rest she had heard and, so far as she could tell, summed up by one of the maidservants she had earlier heard in the solar, exclaiming still on a variation of her theme, 'And think! They've left him loose all this time! It's a wonder it hasn't come to this before. It's a wonder it hasn't. And it could have been anyone he killed. It could have been any of us!'

'And could still be one of us,' the man she talked to said. 'Think on it. They say he takes on the strength of fifteen men when the demon takes hold of him. How likely is he to be held by those little chains and that door there and Deryk? The sooner he's gone the better.'

'They say Sire Benedict blessed the chains with holy water, to be sure they'd hold,' another woman said. She had serving dishes stacked in her hands and was probably meant to be clearing the table.

'And how much good do you think Sire Benedict's holy water is going to do against a demon that can murder a man in a chapel?' the man scoffed. 'If it wills it, Master Knyvet'll pull the chains out of the wall and burst the door and go where he pleases, and where will we be then?'

Frevisse had managed to hear that much by taking more time than needed to edge around them on her way to the door, but now she had heard enough. With the talk going that way, there would be no satisfying folk until Lionel was as harshly, straitly confined as could be managed, with assurances he would be kept that way. Nothing said about the infrequency of his attacks, or that there was warning of them, or that he had never harmed anyone before would make any difference. Even what she had presently in his favour was no more than would give the crowner momentary pause before he completed the condemnation.

She knocked at the Knyvets' chamber door. The maidservant came in answer and turned to say into the room who it was, and Edeyn called out, 'Come in. I pray you, come in.'

She was seated at the window and did not rise, saying with an apologizing smile as Frevisse entered, 'I'm strictly told to rest, to stay at ease and not tire myself by even so much as pacing the room.'

'Is your childing that' – Frevisse looked for a word and chose – 'delicate?'

'So much as I can tell, the child is well and so am I. It's my husband who frets, I suppose because it's the most he can do about the baby and me for now.'

She was speaking with what Frevisse thought was a feigned lightness, as if she had some thought of how she wanted to seem but could not quite carry it off. Her attempt was gallant, though, and Frevisse, who had been surprised to see Giles was not there, asked, to keep the conversation going, 'But Master Giles isn't here?'

'It makes him restless to be closed in,' Edeyn said. 'We ate and then he went out. To the church, I think. And he hopes to talk to Lady Lovell this afternoon. Have you heard when the crowner can be expected?'

The last question betrayed that she was not as settled as she was trying to seem. There had not been time for any messenger even to reach the crowner, let be bring back word of when he might be there. Carefully Frevisse answered, 'There's no word at all yet.' Then she asked because she could not let the matter go, 'May I talk to you of Master Knyvet?'

'Of Lionel?' Edeyn's voice ached somewhere between hurt and gladness. 'Have you seen him again? How is it with him?'

'I saw him just before dinner. He isn't eating but that will pass. Otherwise he's well.'

'Except in his mind where the pain must be near to over-whelming him,' Edeyn returned.

Taken off guard again by one of Edeyn's shifts that showed how much more there was to her than her young, sweet face and pleasant manners, Frevisse returned as directly, 'Except in his mind.' Recovering and wanting to counter the bleakness that admission brought to Edeyn's face, she added, 'Fidelitas is still with him.'

'Then he still has a friend,' Edeyn said.

'At least two,' Frevisse agreed, 'counting you.'

'Counting me,' Edeyn echoed. But the brightness was gone from her face again as she added bitterly, 'For all the good that I can do him.'

'You can maybe do some good. There's something I'm wondering and you may know enough about him to tell me.'

The maid made a negative sound from across the room, but Edeyn brushed a hand in her direction, dismissing her to silence, and said, intent on Frevisse, 'I'm not the one who thinks I'm in need of being treated like Venetian glass. Ask me what you will.'

'What happens to Lionel when an attack comes on him? What does he do?'

'He falls.' Edeyn answered without hesitation, but her voice low and her eyes on Frevisse's face as if to gauge her reaction. 'He simply falls. It's almost as if he's died, he's so suddenly not there. Then his body begins to jerk and twitch – his head and arms and legs and body all at once – and it's horrible because *he* isn't doing it, he isn't there at all, it's all something else making it happen to him. And then he – then it all stops, sometimes with one huge spasm, sometimes not, and he's just left lying there unconscious and not moving until eventually he rouses and is himself again, only tired and a little dazed for a while.'

She had moved a little while she talked, sketching gestures that were not her own, but Frevisse was not sure how much they were like what Lionel actually did and she asked carefully, 'Just how wildly does he fling about in that part of the attack?'

Edeyn made a widened swing of her arm and rolled her head

from side to side. The maid made a distressed sound. Edeyn ignored her and said, 'Like that. A little more violently and his legs with it, not so controlled, but much like that.'

'Nothing more than that?'

'Not anymore. It used to be they'd try to hold him quiet when he was attacked. As many men as could be called, they'd hold on to him, to try to keep him still. Then Martyn found out that that made it worse, as if the demon fought harder if he was fought against. Since then there's been only Martyn doing only what needs to be done to keep Lionel from hurting himself, and the attacks are far easier.'

'How long has it been that way?'

'Oh, years now. Since before I married Giles.'

'And how do you know so exactly what happens in them?'

Edeyn hesitated, then confessed, 'I was there once when an unwarned one came on him. It was in the solar, of an evening after supper, with only him and Martyn and me there. Giles was gone. As soon as it started, the servants all left.'

Across the room her maid made a denying sound.

'Except for Nan,' Edeyn corrected and managed a smile. 'She wouldn't leave because I wouldn't. Afterward Martyn told Lionel that I went when everyone else did, as soon as he collapsed, and that I'd seen nothing else, but that wasn't true. He lied to keep Lionel from feeling worse over it than he did, and since Lionel never asked me directly, I never had to lie to him.'

'About staying there?' Frevisse asked.

'Yes.'

'But you would have lied to him if he had asked?'

'He didn't want me to be there. He doesn't want me to know how it is with him. He would have been unhappy knowing I knew. So I would have lied to him, yes.' She said it simply, not so much defiant as completely certain, beyond any doubt or hesitation.

'So you stayed,' Frevisse said. 'Why?' Though she thought she knew.

'Because I wanted to know exactly how it is with him when it happens, not have it left to my imagining. Can you think what sort of things I could imagine, knowing as little as he and Martyn ever say about them?'

Frevisse did not have to think about what Edeyn might imagine. She had heard enough today alone of what people could conjure up to suppose what worse could be imagined. But that was not all of it and she asked, 'But why did you want to know more?'

For the second time Edeyn hesitated. Her young face firmed, showing something of the woman she might be growing toward, someone stronger than the child she had seemed when Frevisse first saw her along the road, bright with lighthearted talk and riddles. 'Because what if one of the attacks came without warning, the way that one had – they do sometimes – and when Martyn wasn't there? Or—' She paused, making a visible effort to steady herself enough to go on. 'Or what if something happened to Martyn? He was the only one who knew what to do for Lionel. If I knew, then there would at least be me as well. But I never thought ... it would be like ... this.'

'You care—' Frevisse found she had nearly said 'for Lionel.' She changed it to, '—about Lionel.'

'He's kind and good, far more than he might be, considering how it is with him. And he's clever. He and Martyn together were so ...' She stopped, needing to deal with the pain of knowing there would never be Lionel and Martyn together again, nor probably ever even Lionel as things now were.

Frevisse thought she had kept her own face controlled, but Edeyn read something in it, faintly smiled, and said, 'I know. It's all right. Lady Lovell warned me long since to be careful, that people might misthink my friendship, but that's all it's been. Friendship. Lionel has been so much alone except for Martyn.'

And Edeyn was equally alone, Frevisse suddenly thought.

Because Giles might be company but hardly a friend to her, or to anyone, in Frevisse's opinion.

'And your husband doesn't misthink it?' she asked.

'Giles? No.' Edeyn said it with unalloyed confidence. 'He's sure of me.' As sure as she was of herself.

But the heart could be a treacherous thing, going where it was not intended or expected to go. Frevisse wondered if Edeyn knew that well enough to guard against it happening to her; and wondered if Giles had wondered the same thing. But it was not a matter that should concern her and she asked, returning to her reason for being there, 'The attack the other day, in the afternoon, it was as usual?'

'From what Martyn said, yes. It was one of the small ones that come before a great attack. Nothing out of the ordinary, no. Martyn would have said, I think, if it was otherwise. Or Giles would have.'

'Your husband saw it, too?' Frevisse did not try to hide her surprise. She had had the distinct impression Giles found anything to do with Lionel's affliction repulsive. 'That wasn't usual for him, was it?'

Except when her emotion or memory slowed her, Edeyn had been answering readily. Now a – not wariness but questioning of her own – was in her voice as she said slowly, 'No.' Not as if she was reluctant to answer but as if following a thought of her own while she did. 'Giles stays as far from Lionel as he can when we know an attack is coming.'

'But he didn't the other afternoon.'

'No.' Edeyn had been staring at the floor, into her own thoughts. Now she looked back to Frevisse and asked, too low for Nan across the room to hear, 'Why are you asking all this?'

Frevisse abruptly realized that Edeyn had early judged her questions were from more than prying curiosity and that if she had not, she would not have answered them anything like so readily, so openly. In return for Edeyn's trust in her, she answered straightly, 'Because Lady Lovell has given me permission to ask things, to be sure we understand all there is to understand about Martyn's death.'

Something that was too wary to be called hope stirred in the girl's face. Frevisse rose before it could form into something more and said, 'By your leave, may I ask your maid something?'

Edeyn, already halfway to a question of her own, caught herself back, too well mannered to push where she had been put aside. 'Surely.'

She would have called the maid to them, but Frevisse rose and went to her across the room. The woman curtsied and Frevisse asked, since there seemed no subtle way to bring a conversation around to it, 'Did you find out why Master Giles made such a mess of his chest this morning?'

She would have been hard put to say why she was asking that, except that it was another odd thing among odd things and it was oddness that she was looking for, things that did not fit into the simple explanation of Martyn's death, since that no longer seemed so simple.

The maid's indignation instantly kindled. 'For his other shoes. Would you believe it? He was looking for his other pair of shoes.'

'His shoes?' Frevisse echoed, carefully hiding how much the answer jarred against her thoughts.

'He couldn't find the shoes he'd worn yesterday. They should have been right with his clothes where they were put last night but they weren't, he said, and while we were gone – his man and I – to fetch the hot water – if you don't do it yourself, it's brought half warm and he won't tolerate that for himself and Mistress Edeyn and then – well, it saves trouble to just go for it ourselves and have done with it. But today while we're gone he's up and wants to dress and can't find his shoes and digs through his chest for his other pair, and we still don't know where his others went to and there'll go on being trouble over that until it's settled, let me say.'

'The shoes he wore yesterday. Those are what are missing?'

The maid agreed emphatically they were.

His shoes. Could it be that simple?

Giles had long since made a habit of approaching doors with as little sound as possible. There was frequently much to be heard that way, and even when there was not, it was worth the look on people's faces when he was suddenly, unexpectedly there.

This time it was his own turn to be surprised, coming in to find not only Edeyn and that idiot Nan but the tall nun, too. Judging by their expressions as they turned toward the door, he had missed something he might well have liked to hear; but whatever it had been, they had finished saying it before he was in hearing. They had even been, unbelievably enough, considering there were three females there, silent.

Now the problem was how to be rid of the nun. Except for a little dealing over final details, he had won. The thing had gone as he had wanted it to and he was not in the mood for holiness. He wanted celebration, and though he would have to wait for it, he did not mean to wait in any such dull company as this nun's with her long, unamusing face.

So he gave her no more than a curt nod, crossed to Edeyn and deliberately took her hand to kiss it lingeringly, looking in her eyes while he did, before asking, 'Have you been in talk long, love? You shouldn't tire yourself.'

'It's been good to have Dame Frevisse's company. She's been to see Lionel and came to tell me how he does.'

'Has she?' Giles looked across at the nun with an inward grin of understanding. She was here seeking news, straight and simple. Fodder for all the busy tongues. So let her feed if that was what she was craving. Why should he have all the pleasure of Martyn's death? Another week or so and she would be back in her man-forsaken nunnery but with better tales to tell than she had hoped for when she left, that was sure. With a regretful shake of his head, he said, 'The mood against Lionel is ugly around the manor. No one likes that he was left loose among them so long, now that he's known to be so dangerous.'

'He isn't—' Edeyn began.

Giles turned a half-pitying, half-admonishing look on her and refrained from saying the obvious. Her face flushed a dark red and she ducked her head away from his eyes, telling she understood him. He smiled back at the nun. 'How is it with my cousin?'

'Not well. He's taking the death hard.'

'Well he ought. It will take him time to come to terms with what he's done and how things will have to be now. But it could be guessed it might come to this. Gravesend took advantage of his place, and no matter how my cousin tolerated it because he had to, somewhere inside him the anger must have been growing until this time when his frenzy took him, he struck back. He gave the demon its way and it gave him his. That's all. A pity in its way. I would have been satisfied to see Gravesend sent packing down the road rather than down to Hell.'

'You've worried this would happen, then,' the nun said.

'Not this precisely.' There was hardly better sport to be had then leading people to the conclusions he wanted them to have and this woman was ready to go wherever he led. 'But something. Not even Lionel could put up with the fellow much longer. If he chose to let his demon do the striking, well.' He spread his hands to show himself both helpless in the matter and forgiving. 'I'll do the best for Lionel that I can when he's in my keeping.'

'He needs clean clothing and a chance to wash,' the nun said.

'I'll see about it.' Her meddling was unsubtle but in this case helpful. Apparent concern on his cousin's behalf would give him excuse to talk with Lady Lovell and he had been wanting that, to be sure she still meant to go the way he had set her. He too often found it was one thing to put people on a course and another to keep them there, especially with women.

Still bent on everything she could glean from him, the nun asked, 'What happens to your cousin when he's attacked?'

Giles had told this often enough today that it was beginning to bore him, but it would not hurt to make it clear to one more person, especially since she seemed to be more able to talk at ease with Lady Lovell than he had ever yet managed. He shaped his face to regret and pain to show how difficult it was for him to speak of it and said, 'He goes wild. He flings about, arms and legs in all directions. His body wrenches one way and another. He kicks and foams. Five men can't hold him, the demon is that strong in him. And the sounds. God forbid you ever have the misfortune to hear what comes out of his mouth when the fiend is in him.'

'But if it's that way with him, how could he possibly have been able to kill a man?' the nun asked.

Giles deepened his look of regret and added worry. 'What I'm afraid of is that the demon may be gaining the upper hand with him. If that's true, it will all be the worse with him from now on and danger to anyone who's with him when the demon takes hold.'

'But at least there's warning when an attack is coming. His hand.'

If she were half so eager at her prayers as she was at questions, she must be well on her way to sainthood by now; but she had given him another opening and he used it. 'That's been a blessing, right enough, but the warning doesn't always come and now that he has a death on his hands, there may be nothing for it but to keep him confined all the time.'

'Oh, no—' Edeyn began, but Giles closed a hand hard over her nearest one, warning her against whatever half-witted protest she had been about to make.

'If it has to come to that, it has to,' he said. 'Do you want to risk him killing someone else? Think on it, my heart. If I can convince Lord Lovell I should have him in my keeping, at least he'll be with people who know him, care about him. But he'll have to be kept close even then, for your sake, for the child's sake. For everyone's safety, including Lionel's.'

Edeyn bent her head, acknowledging he had the sorry right of it. He appreciated that about her. A stupid wife would have been troublesome, but Edeyn was clever enough to grasp a thing if he made it plain to her and did not think herself so clever as to argue with him. She did what he wanted her to do, when he wanted her to do it, and knew how to keep her mouth shut; and all of that was more than could be hoped for from this nun who talked too much and did not know when she ought to leave.

But Edeyn was useful that way, too. He squeezed her hand again so she would know how he wanted her to answer while he touched her face gently with his other hand and said, 'You look pale. Should you lie down awhile? It's not been a good day.'

Obediently, with only the quickest little glance at the nun, she said, 'You may be right. I … could lie down, I suppose.'

'There's my good girl. You'll pardon us, I hope?' he added pointedly at the nun.

She took the hint, which was almost more than he had hoped for, made her farewell, and left. Giles loosed Edeyn's hand, not caring whether she lay down or not. She did not need to so far as he could tell, and he was less concerned over her than annoyed at the effort it had cost him to be rid of that fool nun. 'What was she here for? To hear all about Lionel so she could tattle it to anyone who'll listen to her, I suppose. What sort of things did she ask?'

'Nothing in particular,' Edeyn answered.

But Nan said with her, so that Giles nearly missed it, 'Your shoes.'

Giles turned on her with narrowing eyes. 'My shoes?'

'The ones that are lost,' Edeyn answered. 'We haven't found them yet or understood how they could be so lost, here in the room.'

'Servants too careless to remember what they've done, or too dishonest to admit to their idiocy, that's how you explain it. How did she come to be asking about them at all, come to that?'

He tried to make it casual but he wanted the answer, and when neither of them gave it to him, he snapped, 'How did shoes come into your conversation? Nan?'

The maid bit her lip, confused because she did not know how angry he was going to be and frightened of what might come because of it. Servants knew enough to be afraid of him, and they knew enough to answer as fast as might be, and after a desperate glance at Edeyn who would be no help if she knew what was good for her, Nan gabbled, 'It's just she was in here this morning while I was putting your chest to rights and I told her I didn't know why it was messed because I didn't. Then just now she asked me if I'd found out why and I had, so I told her.'

God save him from women's tongues. There would be no harm come of her having said so much, but he wished to the devil she had not said it at all. They would never find the shoes he had worn last night. By now they were buried in river mud or, even if they mischanced to be found, were not identifiable as his, and after that while in the river no one would likely be able to tell the stain on the right one's sole was blood.

That had annoyed him, and that it was no one's fault but his own had annoyed him more. He had been so intent on the pleasure of killing Martyn he had forgotten, when he shoved him forward across Lionel, that he needed to put the dagger in Lionel's right hand and Lionel's right hand had been under Martyn. So he had had to straddle over Lionel for a grip on Martyn's shoulders, to pull him back and roll him sideways to clear Lionel's hand, and when he did, he had slid his right foot into some of the blood and not known it until he had put his foot down again as he dropped Martyn and found it sticky on the floor.

So the shoes had had to go. It had not been much problem to hide their soft leather inside the front of his full-cut houpelande this morning, and when all the first shrieking and jabbering over Martyn's death were done, he had only had to go for a walk to the river gate across the yard, watch the water flow awhile, and then take a moment when no one would see him to slip them into the water. He was sure of them, but for just now, for just this while, he would rather shoes were not thought upon by anyone or, more especially, not talked of by tongue-wagging nuns.

But the more he made of it, the less readily they would forget it, so he shrugged with a disgusted look, as if he had never heard anything so stupid in his life, and flicked a hand at Nan to find something useful to do while he turned back to Edeyn.

Chapter 19

IN THE GREAT hall the third person Frevisse asked was able to tell her that Dame Claire was gone out into the garden with most of Lady Lovell's damsels.

'And Lady Lovell?' Frevisse asked.

'Still at work, my lady. There's manor court tomorrow and she's always more to do before that. So she'll know at least as much as the folk she's judging, she says.'

Frevisse thanked the man and betook herself out to the garden, glad of a reason to be outside again and away from her questions, even if only for a little while.

Not that she could truly escape her questions; but she had discovered that if she put them aside awhile, the answers were sometimes waiting for her when she came back to them. The trouble now was that although she thought she had the answer to what had seemed wrong about Martyn's death, she had no way of proving what she thought. A while in the garden might be the respite that she needed.

Coming out of the shadowed passageway, she found the pleasaunce empty of anyone. Formal garden and greensward under the trees were alike quiet, unpeopled, and she wondered where the women had gone instead of here. Then she heard music from beyond the arbour walk, a lighthearted turn on a psaltery, and in no great haste, enjoying her momentary solitude, she made her way to the arbour's shaded way and through it to the rose garden where the rose-trellised cream stone walls held in the warm, mild afternoon sunlight.

Most of Lady Lovell's damsels, the boy Harry, and his sister were there. The children were sitting on the path, rolling a leather ball back and forth between them, and a few of the older women were sitting with their sewing in their laps on the grassy bench that followed the wall, but in the centre of the garden a woman was seated on the edge of the fountain, her dark red skirts spread around her, playing with clever fingers on the psaltery laid in her lap while the rest of the women and girls – Luce among them – circled her hand in hand in a quick-footed, laughing dance.

Frevisse paused, watching. It had been a long while since she had danced and she had no inclination to it now, but it was a pleasure to watch the others' delight in it. It was a simple dance, a few steps sideways leftward, then a few steps sideways rightward, then more steps leftward, a clap of hands, a swirl of skirts as each dancer spun in her place, and then the sideways steps again. Simple, except that with each repetition the lady played a little faster than she had the time before it. Only a little faster but the pace steadily quickening as it was repeated over and over, faster and faster, feet beginning to tangle with skirts and dancers with each other until, breathless, laughing, unable to go on, the circle fell apart.

The lady with the psaltery flourished the tune to a triumphant end. Most of the dancers sank to the grass where they were and the others scattered to the grassy benches, everyone in happy talk. Luce, laughing and breathless like the rest, waved to Frevisse across the greensward. Frevisse smiled in return, but her mind was following a thought the dance had raised. Had it been like that for Giles? Had he started with small meannesses, ones as uncomplicated and simple as the first steps of that dance? No need to think about them much, or plan. They would have just come, as the steps had come with the music in the dance, easy and pleasant. For surely Giles took pleasure in what he did.

Why? Because unkindness was easier than kindness? Because it was more satisfying in the power that it gave him over others? Yes, that likely was it. See, I can make you hurt. You weren't hurting and now you are. I did that. That's how powerful I am.

And the more hurt one could give, the more powerful one was.

That was a lie, of course. The willingness to hurt was not power, it was weakness, because joy, even happiness, was a much more difficult thing to give than pain. Pain was the weakling's way of dealing with the world. Giles had probably slipped from one small meanness to another, each one growing larger, no one's feelings mattering except his own as the devil played him along the way, faster and faster like the steps in the dance, unkindness growing into cruelty, cruelty into ... what?

'Dame Frevisse.'

She had been too intent on her own thinking to notice Dame Claire sitting an arm's length aside from her at the end of the grassy bench beside the arbour's arched way into the rose garden. Embarrassed at her absentmindedness – no, her other-mindedness – Frevisse joined her, no need for greeting between them and her mind already going back to Giles until Dame Claire asked, 'Don't you want to know what I found out?'

Frevisse tried to remember what it was Dame Claire had been supposed to learn and remembered and said, 'There was no blood on anybody's shoes, was there?'

'No.' Dame Claire contained a smile to the corners of her mouth. 'But how could you be so sure?'

'Because the shoes Master Giles wore yesterday are missing.'

The dancers were standing up again, demanding a slow measure this time while the psaltery player protested her fingers needed longer rest than this. Their friendly argument filled up the space of Dame Claire's silence, until she finally said, 'And you think that means – what?'

Frevisse held her answer, feeling at it before she said more carefully than she might have, 'I think that it is an uncomfortable chance that I saw what could have been part of a bloody footprint between the bodies and that Master Giles's shoes should choose today to go missing.'

'And you think Giles was there when Martyn was killed, or afterward sometime, and chose to say nothing about it?'

Frevisse, gazing down at her hands folded in her lap, did not answer that.

So low even Frevisse could barely hear her, Dame Claire said, 'You think it was Giles killed Martyn, don't you?'

Still looking at her hands, Frevisse moved her head down in a single nod.

'But all you have against him are his missing shoes and a possible footprint,' Dame Claire pointed out. 'And the footprint is gone so we can't be sure it was a footprint and we can't see if there's any blood on Master Giles's shoes. In brief, you have nothing.'

'We have a likelihood,' Frevisse said.

'We have a likelihood that's very possibly grown from your dislike of him.'

'I haven't—'

'You do dislike him.'

'And so do you.'

'But I'm not looking to find him a murderer. You've taken against him the way you take against Domina Alys—'

'With good reason in both cases!'

'In her case you maybe take more against her than you should, you're so utterly against her. In his case you've taken against him more than any evidence warrants.'

Frevisse bit back a sharp reply to that. The music and dancing had begun again. So long as they kept their faces neutral and their voices down, no one was likely to heed what they were saying. She waited until she was sure of her face and voice before she said, 'He's lied and lied again about his cousin. He's lied about the way Lionel's fits take him, to make it seem more likely he would be frenzied enough to kill. He's lied about how it was between Lionel and Martyn....'

'He knows how it was between them far better than you can after hardly two days.'

Dame Claire was being reasonable, but knowing that did not stop Frevisse's surge of impatience. 'He *lies*. His wife says one thing and he says flatly the opposite.'

'Then maybe she's the liar, not him.'

'Edeyn?' Frevisse put all her disbelief into that. 'Just now, in their chamber, before he came in, she told me how it is when a fit comes on Lionel. Then Giles came in and told me a different tale, and I saw her face while he did. She hardly believed what she was hearing.'

'Or she wanted you to think so.'

Frevisse started to reply but stopped herself, trying to see the matter as Dame Claire did. What might have been a footprint, now gone. Missing shoes. Her dislike of Giles fed by her certainty that he was both cruel and a liar. Giles's version of Lionel's fits against Edeyn's and – this Dame Claire did not know – the very fact that Edeyn knew so much when she was not supposed to showed she was willing to lie, to Lionel if no one else. There was nothing there to put before a crowner and expect him to appeal a man.

Into her hesitation, Dame Claire urged gently, 'And consider that it may after all have been Lionel indeed. Lionel believes it.'

'If I have to consider someone other than Giles, there's Petir, the dismissed servant. He might be lying when he claims to think it was more Giles's doing than Martyn's that he lost his place. Though I doubt his brain could stretch so far to manage a lie like that.'

'If it could stretch to murder, it could stretch to lying,' Dame Claire pointed out. 'You have to see him as a possibility. There could be others. At least look for them.'

'Who? Who except Giles gains from it?'

'What does it gain Giles?' Dame Claire returned. 'He doesn't gain from killing Martyn. He'll only inherit if Lionel is dead. If he were going to kill anyone, he would have killed Lionel, not Martyn.'

'And be the first one suspected because he was the one with most to immediately gain from Lionel's death?' Frevisse had already thought through that possibility. 'No. Kill Martyn and make it seem Lionel's doing and gamble on the very great likelihood that, since Lionel's lands can't be forfeit because he acted in a kind of madness, they'll be given into his own hands as the heir. This way, he's rid of Martyn – he loathed Martyn – is virtually rid of Lionel, whom I doubt he likes any better, and will likely have the Knyvet lands for his own. That's a great deal of profit from one murder, a profit I can see Giles being willing to gamble for. A worse gamble would be for anyone else to bet on Lionel living very long once Giles has the keeping of him.'

'You've just been arguing it wouldn't serve him to murder Lionel.'

'There are ways enough for an ill-kept prisoner to die without leaving proof it was outright murder. And if ill treatment isn't enough or Giles's patience runs out, there are always poisons or else simple starvation that's claimed to be a wasting sickness when the crowner comes. Giles won't stick at a second death when the first has been so easily, safely, profitably done.'

'But there's still no proof he's done any murder at all,' Dame Claire insisted. 'Say what you will, believe what you will, there's still no proof that Giles had any hand in Martyn's death!'

Frevisse bit back a sharp reply to that because, hate though she might to admit it, Dame Claire was in the right.

Into her hesitation, Dame Claire urged gently, 'You have to consider that Lionel did it indeed.'

Stubbornly Frevisse answered, 'Lionel in the kind of frenzy Giles described or in the sort of attack on him that Edeyn tells of, could never have slit anyone's throat so neatly. And Martyn would never have had his back to him.'

'Maybe that part of the attack was over. Maybe he was fully quieted and Martyn could have been turned away because there was nothing to watch, because he thought it was over, but the demon brought Lionel's body up and killed him then.'

Frevisse shook her head, refusing that.

More strongly Dame Claire said, 'Think on it. Consider it a possibility. Remember, we don't know what happened last night. The demon may very well have changed its ways and have taken Lionel differently than it ever has before.'

Staring at her hands clenched together in her lap, Frevisse said, 'I can find it easier to believe that Giles did it than that Lionel's demon has changed its ways.'

'That's because you dislike Giles even more than you do Lionel's demon. That colours your judgement, the way your dislike of Domina Alys colours your feeling toward everything she does. I can see it,' she went on quickly, cutting off Frevisse's quick reply to that, 'because it's been true of me, too. These days since we left St Frideswide's I've been bringing myself to face that, so I can better bend myself to obedience when we go back. We both have to remember to judge not or we may be judged.'

'It must be easier for you than for me to forget what Domina Alys is like,' Frevisse said tersely. 'And you'd better consider that it's better to judge and be sure your judgement is fair than to leave the world to go down in chaos and unjustice because you didn't dare to judge.'

'The soul's salvation doesn't depend on our judging others.'

'The salvation of someone else's soul might!'

They had forgotten to mind their voices. Now the music faltered and there was giggling from player and dancers, bringing Frevisse and Dame Claire abruptly back to realization that they were not alone and had been, at least at the last, overheard. Still too angry to be embarrassed, and angry enough that she knew she had better leave before she said more, Frevisse rose, turned her back on the other women, dropped her voice to Dame Claire's hearing only, and said, 'Even if I can't prove anything, I can tell Lady Lovell what I suspect and hope that influences her judgement enough to keep Lionel out of Giles's hands.'

'You'll likely influence her to think you're a fool,' Dame Claire hissed back.

'Better a fool than a coward!' Frevisse snapped and left her.

Chapter 20

THE PROBLEM WAS one Giles had failed to consider ahead of
the time. How exactly should he act now, with having a
murderer for cousin and needing to deal with that and the problems that came with it? No one would expect particular grief
from him over a servant, so Martyn's death was no trouble
beyond a few pointed comments concerning his insolence. A
murdering cousin was another matter, and Giles rather thought
he had talked too much at the beginning; but everyone else had
been equally talking and welcomed what he could add and so it
had probably not been noticed out of the ordinary. Besides, he
had used it as a chance to make it clear how dangerous Lionel was
and in need of close confinement. Now it was probably better to
begin emphasizing more strongly than he had his concern for
Lionel's well-being.

Lady Lovell could be worked on that way, being a woman. Her
husband had entrusted too much authority to her over the years
so that she tended to trust her own mind, but that could be
allowed for, and since Lord Lovell listened to her, she was worth
the trouble needed to influence her.

She had had the problem wearing at her the whole day now.
She would be tired and willing to listen to him if he offered to
ease the matter for her. That was why he had deliberately waited
until now to approach her, in the pause before supper when she
was with her women in the pleasaunce, enjoying the day's end.

Edeyn had wanted to come out, complaining she was tired of being inside. She wanted to see Lionel, too, to be sure for herself he was no worse than she had been told. Under excuse of worry for her in her condition, Giles had refused her both. He was beginning to find her attachment to Lionel tedious. He fully intended for her to see Lionel but not until Lionel was sufficiently broken and he himself had leisure to enjoy the scene, not now when he had other things to hand.

He took his time going to Lady Lovell where she sat under the birch trees on the greensward. Most of her women, a few squires, and some of the household knights who had not gone with Lord Lovell were there around her, and even the tall nun who had been with Edeyn. In fact the nun had Lady Lovell in talk, probably trying to woo money for her nunnery out of her. He strolled by various paths among the formal garden beds, giving greeting to the few women walking there but absentmindedly, as if he were in brooding thought, to let them see how deeply he was troubled. Only when he walked long enough to be sure he had been noticed across the greensward as well did he turn his way toward Lady Lovell, who was still in talk with that damned nun.

He edged among the seated, lounging gentlemen and ladies, paused to talk with some, receiving their regrets and comments so he could reply with troubled gratitude to show how burdened he was with what had come on him. When he finally reached Lady Lovell, she gave him only a look and a nod for greeting, indicating she meant to go on talking with that idiot nun for a while longer.

Their voices were too low for him to hear any of what they said, so to seem at ease and not appear to eavesdrop, he sat down on his heels beside Sir Rohard. The old dotard had been a knight since Agincourt twenty-odd years ago and was showing his years by a tendency to talk of nothing but his past experiences. Even a present murder was worth nothing more than a passing mention of sympathy before it led him on to talk of one he remembered in Calais twenty years ago. Giles pretended to listen. Sir Rohard needed no more than an occasional vague sound from his listeners, to show they were still awake, Giles supposed, and that left Giles free to watch Lady Lovell's conversation for a chance to break in there.

The chance did not come as quickly as he wanted. He could still catch nothing of what they said, but as his glances away from Sir Rohard became more frequent he realized the two women were likewise sometimes glancing at him and that their glances were ... he found the word he wanted: assessing.

He did not like to be assessed, particularly by women, particularly by Lady Lovell, and especially just now. Women's attempts at intelligence invariably led to trouble. What was the nun playing at? he suddenly wondered. Now he came to think about it, he had seen her too many places today, and God knew where else she had been. To see Lionel for one, and then to see Edeyn, and that was one place too many right there.

He remembered the silence there had been when he had walked into the room, and the looks she and Edeyn had turned on him. It was after that Edeyn had begun to mention that she wanted to see Lionel and be restless at staying in the room. What had the nun said to her? And what was she saying now to Lady Lovell?

He tried to listen past the drone of Sir Rohard's voice and caught instead a piece of the conversation between the two women beyond him sitting beside and a little behind him. '... over soles,' the younger was saying.

His attention abruptly refocused, Giles leaned slightly their way to hear them better.

'There in the rose garden?' the older woman asked. 'They were actually arguing?'

'Trying not to look angry, mind you, being two nuns and all, but angry they were and arguing.' The girl was holding in giggles. 'Over soles. That one' – Giles had shifted his head slightly to see them out of the corner of his eye. The girl tipped her head toward the nun with Lady Lovell – '… turned so angry over it, she stood up and left the other sitting there.'

They both smothered laughter behind their hands. Sir Rohard finished firmly, 'And that was the end of that. There'd be no more rebels coming out of that French village.'

With only the vaguest thought of what the old fool had been babbling about, Giles said at random, 'And that wasn't the only time for you either, was it?'

'Not by any means.' Sir Rohard drew willing breath and went on while Giles tried to hear what else the women had to say, only to find their talk had gone on to something about one of the squires. His mind turned restlessly back. What had the nun said about soles that made the other nun angry? She had been asking about his shoes this afternoon, he remembered. She had learned from that fool Nan that they were missing. What else had she learned? What was she playing at and what was she saying to Lady Lovell that had them both so dour-faced? She could not have actually found anything. Not his shoes surely. That was … impossible?

The mere fact that he hesitated on the thought, that he had to pause in doubt at all, infuriated him. There was supposed to be virtually nothing more for him to do but let this thing run its course, until he had Lionel in his keeping. That was the way he had planned it. Now it looked as if it was not going to be that simple after all.

'In those days they hadn't it in their heads yet we'd crush them whenever they rose up,' Sir Rohard was saying.

Giles interrupted him. 'I pray your pardon, but I have to see how it goes with my wife. With everything that's happened today, she's keeping to her bed and it's best if I'm not gone from her too long.'

'Ah, to be sure.' Sir Rohard nodded vague agreement. 'A lovely lady. Of course.'

Giles doubted the old fool even knew who Edeyn was. He rose, bowed briefly to him and toward Lady Lovell who did not see it, being head close to head with that nun, and retreated back toward the house with a more restrained walk than he wanted to have.

There were other ways this could be settled.

But damn to hell people who made complications where there did not have to be any.

Chapter 21

W HEN FREVISSE HAD finished, Lady Lovell sat silently, deep in thought. Her face had always seemed best suited to serenity, and though by now Frevisse knew how readily it could quicken with laughter, it was disconcerting to watch the subtle growth of anger in it as she settled into decision.

'If that has indeed been Master Giles's way,' she said quietly, 'I'll see to it that matters go very ill for him after this.'

'Whether better proof can be found or not?' Frevisse asked.

'If nothing else, by what you've said, he's been unfaithful to his cousin in everything he's done and said today. I doubt you'll be the only one who says so when I ask Master Holt and others what they've heard. At the very least I'm satisfied Giles should have no care of Lionel when this is done. As for the rest, there's not enough for crowner or sheriff to act against him and that's a pity.' Lady Lovell's anger was very deep. 'But you've found enough to make me wary, and my lord husband when I tell him. Do you think there's any chance you can learn more?'

'As things stand now, no.' Frevisse hated to admit that but saw no way around it. After leaving Dame Claire she had paced the garden until her anger had quieted and then set about finding out what else she could in the while before Lady Lovell was free to listen to her. What little she had found out had not been much use.

The question of Petir had been easily taken care of. His fellows in the stable had readily told her that his evening had been spent dicing with them first in the great hall and then in the stables. They had laughed over it because for once he had won more than he lost and had made them go on playing later than they should have. When they had settled to sleep in the loft, Petir had gone to his usual far corner, with no way to the ladder for him except by stepping over four other men and, no, he had never gone out until they all did in the morning because one of them was an especially light sleeper and would have known if he had.

They had been curious at her questions but free enough in their answers that she did not doubt them. Whatever Petir truly felt about Martyn, even if he had lied about not being particularly angry at him, he had had no chance to kill him last night.

She had also tried to learn what was generally thought of Martyn, but there was disappointingly little talk to be had about him and none of it to the bad, either from such servants as she asked or from Master Holt, who had said, 'He was one of the most straightforward men I've ever known, honest, competent. He could have done well for himself almost anywhere and had less burden to bear than he did with Master Knyvet, but that was where his loyalty first was and there he kept it, come what may. What will come now, with him gone and Master Giles likely given charge of everything ... Well, he'll find a steward to his liking but not a better one.'

He had not said more and Frevisse had not pressed him.

Now she had given it all to Lady Lovell, and Lady Lovell was gazing past her with anger-darkened eyes toward the house, the way Giles had gone a while ago, saying musingly, more to herself than Frevisse, 'I've never much cared for Master Giles.'

'But you married Edeyn to him,' Frevisse said before she could stop herself, only barely managing to keep accusation out of her voice.

Lady Lovell looked mildly surprised but not offended. 'It was a good marriage for her, with her dowry none so large nor his property either, but him to have all the Knyvet inheritance someday. I've gathered that they've done reasonably well together. She's seemed happy the few times I've seen her.'

And she had seemed happy when Frevisse first encountered her on the road three days ago; but, seen from now, so much of that happiness had been centred around Lionel and Martyn and their shared laughter. How much of that happiness was left, and how would it fare with only her husband for a source?

Frevisse caught herself on that thought. It was unnecessarily unkind, come out of her own dislike of the man. Dame Claire was maybe right: maybe she did let her likes and dislikes too much influence her reactions to people. But in Giles's case....

She stopped the thought because it was only the beginning of another justification of her dislike of him. Instead she said, 'By your leave, my lady, if you need me for nothing more, I think I should find Dame Claire for our evening prayers now.'

Lady Lovell nodded her agreement. 'But if you think of anything more or learn anything else, come talk to me again.'

Frevisse left her with thanks but little hope. There were simply no more questions she could think to ask of anyone, and all the questions she had asked so far had found her no one else to suspect besides Giles, and against Giles she had nearly nothing except – when all was said and done and fairly faced – her dislike of him that maybe brought her to make more of things than she should.

The manor house rose ahead of her at its most beautiful, she thought, with its stone a rich cream-gold in the late afternoon light. Like the garden well kept and carefully enclosed, it was meant to be a place for living securely, well, and in as much peace as life allowed. But how well, how safely, how much at peace could that life be if rot and danger were not an outward threat but inside of it and growing? There had been murder here, and she was afraid, very afraid, that there was something worse than murder, because the murder was only the final outcome of something deeply wrong. There was a wrongness in Giles, a corruption that would taint everything around him. What if she never proved Martyn's murder against him? Aside from what it meant to Lionel, what would come of Giles left free? Because if Giles could kill as she thought he had killed Martyn – in cold calculation to ruin Lionel – then what other things would he go on to do?

She passed from the sunlight into the shadowed passage to the great hall. Giles's face in the garden while he sat listening to the old knight had been simply a face, polite, a little vacant as the knight had gone on with a story Frevisse doubted Giles wanted to hear, but there had been nothing particular about him, nothing to single him out as anyone apart in mind or manners from anyone around him. But no matter what she could prove or not prove to anyone else, no matter what he *seemed*, Frevisse was certain he was as much a venomed thing as any adder found under any flower in any garden there might be.

Despite what she had thought was her intent to find Dame Claire and go to prayers, she found herself at the foot of the stairs to Lionel's cell, not the stairs to the chapel. Had anyone been to see him at all this afternoon? Quietly she went up the stairs' curve, to stop with surprise in sight of the door because the only guard there was Edeyn, standing with her forehead leaned against the frame, a hand pressed flat to the door's wood, her eyes closed, her lips moving as if she silently prayed.

Because it would be cruel to watch her unaware, Frevisse said, 'Edeyn.'

The girl straightened and faced her, startled but too distracted by her feelings to care she had been seen so vulnerable.

'Where's Deryk?' Frevisse asked. 'The guard who was here.'

Or by now Deryk might have been replaced by someone else. It did not matter. Someone was supposed to be here. But Edeyn answered, 'He left.'

'He left?' Before Frevisse could demand why, there was a

sharp whining and scrabble of claws against the inside of the door, distracting her. 'Fidelitas?' she asked and pushed the door open.

'Don't!' Edeyn cried. 'She'll go—' Fidelitas was a white streak between their skirts, gone down the stairs. Edeyn drew an anguished breath. 'Giles will be so angry! She'll go to Lionel and—'

'To Lionel?' Only the quickest glance was needed to see the room was empty. 'Where's Lionel gone?'

'With Giles—'

'Where? *Why?*' Frevisse interrupted.

'Master Holt gave Giles leave to see to Lionel having a bath and clean clothing. Giles asked him if he could. Giles asked – Giles ... asked—' Edeyn broke off, closed her eyes, and thrust her clenched hands against her forehead, crying out in pain, 'I'm so afraid!'

Frevisse grasped her wrists and pulled her hands down, demanding, 'Where are they?'

'In our chamber!'

'But the servants are still there!'

'No, Giles sent them away. There's no one there!'

No one there to gainsay Giles if he claimed the madness had come back on Lionel and he had had to kill him to defend himself.

The thought came hot and clear and terrifying. Frevisse saw it mirrored in Edeyn's face and knew that whatever barriers Edeyn had made to protect herself against knowing what her husband was were broken by her fear for Lionel. 'We can't leave them alone!' she said fiercely. 'Edeyn, come!'

Giles watched as Lionel fumblingly managed to undress himself. A servant would have been useful for that, or it would have gone faster if Giles helped him; but there could not be a servant here and Giles was not about to touch that blood-filthied clothing. He rose from the edge of the bed impatiently, wanting to pace, but made himself sit back down again. There was time. He could wait.

Lionel was slowly working what had been his white shirt loose from the blood caking it to his side. He had done everything slowly since Giles had fetched him from his cell, as if his mind were not fully there or fully caring. The only swift movement he had made was when they had come into the room and Edeyn had been there despite that Giles had told her to be gone along with the servants. She had started toward Lionel with a soft cry, but Lionel had turned from her to face the wall and stayed there until she left. Giles had enjoyed that. Let that be her last view of Lionel alive – dirty, unshaven, ashamed, covered in Martyn's blood. Let her remember him that way, and dead.

Even with her gone, Lionel had only stood there until Giles had told him to strip. He was taking forever at it. The steam was rising from the filled tub beside him. The water would be tepid by the time he was ready for it. It hardly mattered. Giles had not yet decided exactly when Lionel would die. He had found with Martyn that once it was done, it was done, and the only pleasure left was in remembering. The act itself was so brief, he did not want to waste the pleasure of his anticipation. On the other hand, he could not wait too long; inevitably someone would come to see how they were.

Lionel let the shirt fall and then stood there as if he could not remember he had more to do.

'Your hosen,' Giles said sharply.

Lionel's hands went vaguely toward untying their points.

Maybe it would be better to kill him now. The rate he was not moving, they'd be here to midnight.

A peremptory rap at the door brought Giles up from the bed edge with a curse. 'What is it?' The only answer was another knock, harder. He cursed again. Some fool of a servant who could not follow orders to stay away. He went to jerk open the door. 'What—' he began, but Lionel's cur dodged past him into the room, distracting him. He began a grab for her before he realized it was no servant come with her but that tall nun and, unbelievably, Edeyn. On her at least he could turn his full displeasure.

'I told you—' he started.

The nun looked past him, and he realized he had momentarily forgotten Lionel. It was uncomfortable, not being sure where Lionel was, and Giles swung half away from her, only to find he had withdrawn to a corner and turned away from them. Before Giles could come back on Edeyn, the nun was past him, into the room, and Edeyn with her, gabbling, 'We were going to the chapel. We thought we could—'

He saw the fear in their faces. He was so used to finding out shadings and possibilities of fear on the faces of people that theirs were easy to read, Edeyn most especially, but the nun, too. It was her fault – her with her suspicions – that he had to move faster on the matter of Lionel than he wanted, and now somehow she had infected Edeyn, and sure as misery, they had come to interfere. Who else had the nun persuaded?

The tightening coil of alarm in his chest abruptly loosed, because if the nun had had any real proof against him, there would have been men at the door, not merely whey-faced Edeyn and herself.

But suspicion was enough to make things awkward; and not only could he not afford anything awkward just now, he assuredly did not want Edeyn's suspicions plaguing him afterward.

Therefore there had to be no afterward.

They were inside and Lionel safe for now. There had been no time for planning more than that. Edeyn was talking rapidly, trying to make excuse for their coming, but the cold flicker of Giles's eyes back and forth to their faces warned Frevisse that he understood more by their being here than she had hoped he would.

Ignoring Edeyn, he turned his back on them, shut the door, and stepped aside to push the large wooden chest that sat along the wall scraping across the floor to block the door shut.

Edeyn squeaked to a stop, then asked faintly, 'Giles?'

He did not answer except to go past them to the head of the bed and draw a dagger out from under the nearest pillow. With terrible clarity, Frevisse understood how he had probably made a show for the servants of hiding it there before Lionel was brought in, to make it clear he did not mean to make Martyn's supposed mistake of wearing a weapon around Lionel but establishing that he had it readily to hand. She also understood, even before he had turned around to face them again, exactly what he meant to do with it now. With all three of them dead, he could claim that Lionel had gone into a frenzy, killed Edeyn and her before Giles could stop him, and that Giles had then killed him in defence, rage, and revenge.

'Giles?' Edeyn asked. 'What—?'

Frevisse pushed her backward, putting the bath, the only large thing on their side of the room, between them and Giles as he closed on them. There was no hope of the door. Even if they separated and ran, he would have first one of them and then the other before either of them could shove the chest away from the door. 'Scream, Edeyn!' she ordered, and caught up a towel from the edge of the bath, stretching it between her hands as some sort of shield against the coming dagger thrust. If she could catch the dagger somehow, or tangle Giles's hand, it would mean a moment more for something else to happen, a moment more for her to think of something besides keeping him away from Edeyn.

She never thought of Lionel. She had glimpsed him withdrawn into a corner when they came in and then there had only been time for Giles.

But Edeyn cried out not for help but, 'Lionel!' and he was

suddenly there, unarmed and almost naked but come at Giles from the side, catching him unready. With mingled fury and surprise, Giles retreated, slashing to hold him off, trying to put distance enough between them for a thrust, but Lionel gave him no space, caught his wrist with one hand, his throat with the other. Giles, with the strength of absolute fury, twisted his hand against Lionel's hold, bringing the dagger around to graze across Lionel's collarbone. Blood welled along the line it made. Edeyn at last began to scream in earnest, but Lionel dragged Giles's hand away from himself, and Frevisse flung the towel over the dagger, one fold, two, and three, wrapping it, then jerking it down, backward out of Giles's hand. Giles wrenched out of Lionel's double hold with a sideways twist to follow the dagger as it fell, shoving Frevisse aside with one hand, going for the dagger with the other; but before his fingers closed on it, Fidelitas was there, sinking teeth into his wrist. His yell and Lionel's joined as Lionel shoved a foot into his ribs, staggering him back against the bed. Giles thrust off of it and back at Lionel, but Lionel straightened with the dagger in his hand and drove it hilt-deep into Giles's side.

Edeyn's scream cut off. Giles, his face blank, sank to the floor, gripping Lionel's arm with both hands, the dagger still in his side, Lionel still holding it. Outside someone yelled to know what was happening, then thudded against the door, expecting it to open. It barely yielded, but more men and their voices were joining the first. Two more hard shoves like that one would have them in the room, and what they would see was Lionel over Giles with a dagger in his hand.

'Edeyn!' Frevisse cried. 'Help me!'

Chapter 22

EDEYN UNDERSTOOD AND, as Frevisse caught Lionel by one bare shoulder, she came to catch him by the other, the both of them pulling him back from Giles, Edeyn pleading, 'Lionel! Lionel, leave him!'

As they pulled him away, Giles lost his hold and slumped backward off the dagger, onto the floor, his mouth beginning to twist with the first realization of pain. The dagger still in his hand, Lionel gave only two steps to Edeyn and Frevisse's pulling, staring down at Giles as if unable to see or hear anything but him, until Edeyn grabbed his face between her hands and turned it toward herself, begging, 'Lionel, listen to me. They're going to kill you! Come with me!'

The door gave inches more to another hard push. There were faces there now, able to see in, and the yelling was louder. Lionel flung his head around to stare at them.

'Lionel!' Edeyn begged, and finally he seemed to grasp his danger. As he let Edeyn begin to pull him away toward the farthest corner, Frevisse grabbed the dagger from his hand and threw it across the room, then backed away with him and Edeyn into the corner, with herself and Edeyn between him and the door as the chest gave way to thrusting shoulders.

'Fidelitas!' Lionel called, and she came to him in a leap over Giles's body. He scooped her up into his arms as the door was shoved wide. Frevisse and Edeyn closed together, shielding him from the men now crowding through, coming at him with their daggers out.

'No!' Edeyn cried at them, more fierce than afraid. 'Leave him alone! He hasn't done anything! There's your murderer!' She pointed in fury at her husband on the floor, curled in on his pain. 'He killed Martyn and he tried to kill us! He tried to kill all of us!'

The men stopped, confused by what she said, more confused at the sight of two women defending a nearly naked, blood-marked man with a white dog in his arms. Into their confusion Frevisse said with a desperately feigned calmness, trying to sound reasonable and as if she expected them to be reasonable with her, 'Where's Master Holt? We need him here.' To give them something to do, she added, pointing at Giles, 'He needs help. Can you bring someone?'

Her assumption of authority and their uncertainty decided them. Men turned to explain over their shoulders to those behind them what was going on without being sure they understood it themselves, then to Frevisse's great relief Master Holt was there, forcing his way among them to the front. From everything being said around him, he grasped what was toward, gave order for Giles to be carried out, and as men gathered around to do it, came to where Frevisse and Edeyn still guarded Lionel.

'Giles killed Martyn?' he asked. 'Is that what I understand?'

'And tried to kill us,' Frevisse finished. 'He meant to kill Lionel when he had him alone here, and then claim Lionel had gone into another killing frenzy and he'd done it to defend himself. When Edeyn and I interfered, he turned to kill us, too, meaning to blame it on Lionel, to more justify killing him.'

'And you?' Master Holt demanded of Lionel. 'How is it with you?'

Standing straightly, clear-eyed, Lionel answered, 'Well. Unscathed.' He seemed unaware of the cut on his shoulder. He glanced past Master Holt to where Giles was being carried from the room. 'I hope I've killed him.'

'It will save a deal of trouble if you have,' Master Holt said. He looked at Frevisse. 'Because he did kill Martyn, didn't he?'

She nodded, finding herself suddenly too exhausted for any word. She wanted to sit down before her suddenly weak legs gave out, but beside her Edeyn began to crumble first. Frevisse and Master Holt both reached for her, but Lionel dropped Fidelitas and had Edeyn in his arms before she was fully to the floor. As she clung to him, beginning to cry, he carried her to the bed, laid her gently down, and whispered something only she could hear. She clung to him more closely and he held her tightly in return.

When the while of explanations was over and there had been supper and the manor was settling into evening ways, habits taking hold even in the tide of tonight's talk, Frevisse slipped away from company and questions to the dark garden. The nearer paths were a paleness in what faint light came from over the parlour shutters. Further from the hall there was only starlight under the clear night sky, but that was enough to care for her feet across the greensward among the birch trees to the arbour where she found her way through its deeper darkness to the rose garden and starlight again.

The evening damp was rising, and it was foolish to be out, she knew, but she needed solitude awhile, time for her thoughts to settle and new equilibrium to come. Eased by the silence, she looked up at the sky. So many stars there. Windows into a heaven unimaginably far. So long a way for a soul to go.

She said a prayer for Martyn's soul, wherever on its journey it now was, and brought herself to make another prayer for Giles, whose soul was still in his body but probably not beyond tonight; he was expected to die before dawn. Sire Benedict had already given him Last Rites, so Master Holt had told her. He had tried to talk to him when what could be done for his wound had been done.

'And even now he's raging that everyone's stupidity interfered with what he meant to do. At you in particular for spoiling how cleverly he had managed Martyn's death, and at you and Edeyn and Lionel altogether for crossing him at the end,' Master Holt had said coldly, in anger and disgust. 'He's better off dead, for everyone's sake.'

For everyone's sake but Giles's. The devils that must have haunted him all his life were surely closing in now for the moment when his body could no longer hold his soul; having fallen back into rage, he had forfeited the safety the Last Rites had given him. Lionel's demon had been the more obvious all these years, but Giles's demons were the more deadly when all was said and done, destroying a soul instead of only flesh.

So there would be an end of Giles, and for Lionel and Edeyn a change in everything their lives had been. Edeyn still carried Giles's heir, but when Giles was dead, she would be that most independent of women, a widow, more in control of her own life than had ever been allowed her before. There was no chance of marriage between her and Lionel, not only because he had sworn never to marry but because she had been married to his cousin; man's law and God's barred any closer link between them. But the child to come was equally Lionel's heir: there was a bond they could keep. Whatever they made of that and of whatever else there was between them would come in time's fullness, Frevisse reflected, and all she could give them were her prayers, but those she would give gladly.

And for herself? More prayers because the angry questions there had been between her and Dame Claire were still there to be answered, and the answers had to do with more than only what she had done today. If she had succeeded in meeting Dame Claire's challenge to hold her judgement in check, if she had drawn back instead of going on, it would have cost Lionel his life. If she had stood aside from what she was sure of, Giles would have been able to kill again.

So she could say she had been right. But so had Dame Claire. She had been driven as much by her dislike of Giles as anything else, and the good that had come of it could almost be called happenstance.

Judgement, justice, and fairness all existed. They were supposed to be one and the same, but they were not, not as often as they should be.

And there was what was commonly called common sense that was supposed to be the root of wisdom; but Frevisse had found too often before this that what was common was not necessarily sensible, nor what was sensible necessarily common. Common sense had seemed to make it clear to everyone how Martyn had been killed and common sense had been wrong. Had it been wisdom then that had taken her beyond that into her doubts? Or, as Dame Claire said, only her ill-judgement based on no more than dislike?

She had no answers yet as to what she would do when she was once again in St Frideswide's, confronted with Domina Alys. She had hoped, had prayed she would be able to change, to become more accepting, but she doubted that she had. Not yet. Maybe she would simply have to live it through, finding her way day by day, no overwhelming answer given. Maybe it had to be enough that for here and now something had been made right, that two people had been saved from so much wrong.

The light wind whispering among the rose leaves said there would be rain before morning; the long run of fair days was ended. But in a pause before supper she and Dame Claire had talked and were already agreed there was no reason why they should not go on their way tomorrow, come what may, whatever weather. Assuredly, she was ready.

Author's Note

The Lovell family and their manor of Minster Lovell were not made up for this story. The effigy of Lord Lovell mentioned here is still in the parish church, and the ruins of their lovely manor house can still be visited beside the Windrush River under Wychwood in Oxfordshire. I recommend it.

As for Lionel Knyvet's affliction, epilepsy has been known throughout history. It takes many different forms and is better understood now than ever before, with ways to often control the seizures, but through most of the centuries it was seen as either a mental disease – madness – or else as a spiritual one – possession by either demonic or shamanistic spirits, depending on the culture in which the person lived (and lives; such beliefs persist in many places) – or of course as madness brought on by demonic possession.

In medieval English law, madness was a recognized defence. The legal ramifications of Lionel's supposed crime, given he had apparently committed it while mad, were as compassionate as laid out in the story. Instead of a legally-recognized madman's property being seized into the king's hands and lost after he was found guilty of committing a crime, his property would be held in trust for him, in the hope of him regaining his wits, whereupon his property and his freedom would be restored to him.

Of course the law also includes a warning to beware of someone feigning madness in order to avoid punishment, which

goes to show that human nature holds true through the years –
and that medieval lawyers and juries were no fools.